# From the Pages of
## *The Wonderful Wizard of Oz*

"You are welcome, most noble Sorceress, to the land of Munchkins. We are so grateful to you for having killed the wicked Witch of the East, and for setting our people free from bondage."          (page 22)

While Dorothy was looking earnestly into the queer, painted face of the Scarecrow, she was surprised to see one of the eyes slowly wink at her. She thought she must have been mistaken, at first, for none of the scarecrows in Kansas ever wink.          (page 35)

"No matter how dreary and gray our homes are, we people of flesh and blood would rather live there than in any other country, be it ever so beautiful. There is no place like home."          (page 42)

"I shall take the heart," returned the Tin Woodman; "for brains do not make one happy, and happiness is the best thing in the world."          (page 55)

"If you don't mind, I'll go with you," said the Lion, "for my life is simply unbearable without a bit of courage."          (page 63)

They now came upon more and more of the big scarlet poppies, and fewer and fewer of the other flowers; and soon they found themselves in the midst of a great meadow of poppies. Now it is well known that when there are many of these flowers together their odor is so powerful that anyone who breathes it falls asleep, and if the sleeper is not carried away from the scent of the flowers he sleeps on and on forever.          (pages 78–80)

"You killed the Witch of the East and you wear the silver shoes, which bear a powerful charm. There is now but one Wicked Witch left in all this land, and when you can tell me she is dead I will send you back to Kansas—but not before." (pages 108–109)

This made Dorothy so very angry that she picked up the bucket of water that stood near and dashed it over the Witch, wetting her from head to foot. (page 127)

As the Monkey King finished his story Dorothy looked down and saw the green, shining walls of the Emerald City before them. She wondered at the rapid flight of the Monkeys, but was glad the journey was over. (page 144)

"I am Oz, the Great and Terrible," said the little man, in a trembling voice, "but don't strike me—please don't!—and I'll do anything you want me to." (page 150)

"Can't you give me brains?" asked the Scarecrow.
    "You don't need them. You are learning something every day. A baby has brains, but it doesn't know much. Experience is the only thing that brings knowledge, and the longer you are on earth the more experience you are sure to get." (page 154)

"But I don't want to live here," cried Dorothy. "I want to go to Kansas, and live with Aunt Em and Uncle Henry." (page 174)

Dorothy said nothing. Oz had not kept the promise he made her, but he had done his best, so she forgave him. As he said, he was a good man, even if he was a bad Wizard. (page 182)

When they were all quite presentable they followed the soldier girl into a big room where the Witch Glinda sat upon a throne of rubies. (page 207)

Dorothy now took Toto up solemnly in her arms, and having said one last good-bye she clapped the heels of her shoes together three times, saying, "Take me home to Aunt Em!" (page 211)

# THE WONDERFUL WIZARD OF OZ

*L. Frank Baum*

*Pictures by W. W. Denslow*
*With an Introduction and Notes by J. T. Barbarese*

George Stade
Consulting Editorial Director

**BARNES & NOBLE CLASSICS**
NEW YORK

# BARNES & NOBLE CLASSICS
## NEW YORK

Published by Barnes & Noble Books
122 Fifth Avenue
New York, NY 10011

www.barnesandnoble.com/classics

*The Wonderful Wizard of Oz* was first published in 1900.

Published in 2005 by Barnes & Noble Classics with new Introduction,
Notes, Biography, Chronology, Inspired By, Comments & Questions,
and For Further Reading.

*The Wonderful Wizard of Oz*
ISBN-13: 978-1-59308-221-5
ISBN-10: 1-59308-221-5
LC Control Number 2005920760

Produced and published in conjunction with:
Fine Creative Media, Inc.
322 Eighth Avenue
New York, NY 10001

Michael J. Fine, President and Publisher

Printed in the United States of America
QM
14   16   18   20   19   17   15   13

# L. Frank Baum

When Lyman Frank Baum asked Maud Gage to marry him in 1882, the girl's mother, a pioneering feminist, fiercely opposed the union. She apparently had good reason: The privileged son of a wealthy oilman, Baum led an itinerant life, uncertain of his future career; at the time, he was acting in a touring theatrical production funded by his father. Maud nevertheless went through with the marriage and found her husband to be a passionate, hardworking dreamer. Like his contemporary Mark Twain, Baum would reach the height of literary success only to have its fruits foiled by ill-timed and often fanciful investments.

If character was destiny for Baum, then early aspirations foretold a future in literature. Born in Chittenango, New York, in 1856, Frank spent his childhood on the Baum family estate, where he was given a printing press and created a family newspaper, the *Rose Lawn Home Journal*, with his brother. Despite a congenital heart ailment, Baum was quite active as a young man. He began writing professional newspaper articles, plays, poetry, and even a primer on breeding Hamburg chickens in the years following the American Civil War.

When his father and older brother died in 1887, the family's fortunes declined, and Baum and his wife moved to Aberdeen in the Dakota Territory, where Maud's brothers and sisters were living. Baum started a general store, Baum's Bazaar, where local children gathered for candy and the imaginative stories Baum told for their entertainment. But their generous extensions of credit to drought-plagued ranchers and farmers forced the couple out of business in 1890. An ill-timed foray into newspaper editing and other publishing ventures left them bankrupt and poised for another move, this time to Chicago. To make ends meet, Frank worked as a reporter and, with good success, as a traveling salesman for the glassware company Pitkin and Brooks.

Although Baum's four sons had long enjoyed their father's

fantastical stories, Baum did not publish his tales until *Mother Goose in Prose* appeared in 1897. Its success inspired *Father Goose, His Book* (1899), which was the best-selling children's book of the year. But it was the story of a farm girl named Dorothy, first told to his sons and neighborhood children in 1898, that became an instant success and would endure as a perpetual classic. Published as *The Wonderful Wizard of Oz* in 1900, with illustrations by William Wallace Denslow, Baum's tale flew out of stores and, when it was staged in 1902, sold out theaters from New York to Chicago.

Thrilled by the novel's reception, Baum wrote many sequels to the Oz story and enjoyed considerable financial success. But he also wanted to expand his repertoire beyond stories about Oz. His other books, some published under pen names, include *Queen Zixi of Ix* (1905), *The Fate of a Crown* (1905), and the teen series Aunt Jane's Nieces (1906 through 1915). While these works enjoyed a healthy readership, failed business choices and his audience's insatiable thirst for more Oz stories, kept him writing sequels until his death.

Always the devoted family man, Baum spent his final years living a quiet life in California. The grounds of his house (named Ozcot) were lush with Baum's prize-winning flowers, which he cultivated until heart and gallbladder problems seriously threatened his health. Frank Baum died of a heart attack on May 6, 1919.

# Table of Contents

The World of L. Frank Baum and
*The Wonderful Wizard of Oz*
ix

Introduction by J. T. Barbarese
xiii

THE WONDERFUL WIZARD OF OZ
5

Endnotes
215

Inspired by *The Wonderful Wizard of Oz*
221

Comments & Questions
227

For Further Reading
231

# The World of L. Frank Baum and *The Wonderful Wizard of Oz*

**1856** Lyman Frank Baum is born on May 15 in Chittenango, New York, to Cynthia Stanton Baum and Benjamin Ward Baum. Having made a sizable fortune in oil and other business ventures, Benjamin is able to raise his family of nine children in comfort.

**1861** The American Civil War begins. Benjamin's prospects continue to improve, allowing him to purchase a country mansion outside Syracuse, New York; called Rose Lawn, it has grounds large enough for young Frank to keep a flock of bantam chickens. Frank is a frail child, having been born with a heart ailment that will plague him into adulthood.

**1865** The Civil War ends on April 9, and President Lincoln is assassinated five days later.

**1866** Lewis Carroll's *Alice's Adventures in Wonderland* is published. Baum will later be compared to Carroll because they both wrote about a young female protagonist.

**1868** Frank is sent to Peekskill Military Academy; he loathes the school's exacting discipline and schedule. Louisa May Alcott's *Little Women* is published.

**1870** Frank's ill health allows him to leave Peekskill Military Academy.

**1871** Early interests in writing and journalism lead Frank to create a household newspaper, the *Rose Lawn Home Journal*.

**1873** Jules Verne's *Around the World in Eighty Days* is published.

**1876** Mark Twain's *The Adventures of Tom Sawyer* is published.

**1877** Baum begins writing professional journal articles and becomes involved in the theater.

**1878** With high hopes for a stage career, he begins acting with the Union Square Theatre in Manhattan.

1882   Benjamin Baum funds a theater company for Frank, who
       writes his first play, *The Maid of Arran*. The production,
       with Frank in the lead role, enjoys some critical and com-
       mercial success during its two-year run. Baum marries
       Maud Gage.

1883   Baum and Maud have a child, Frank Joslyn. Robert Louis
       Stevenson's *Treasure Island* is published.

1884   Mismanagement and probable embezzlement by a book-
       keeper cause the theater company to fold. Mark Twain's *Ad-
       ventures of Huckleberry Finn* appears.

1885   Baum sells Baum's Castorine, an axle grease, for his family's
       oil company.

1886   Baum writes his first book, *The Book of Hamburgs*, on the
       breeding and care of Hamburg chickens. Baum's second
       son, Robert, is born.

1887   Benjamin Baum and his oldest son die. With the loss of the
       two competent Baum businessmen, the family's income is
       greatly reduced. Frank and Maud Baum move to Aberdeen
       in the Dakota Territory, where they start a general store.

1890   Baum's third son, Harry, is born. Baum's store fails. Baum
       takes over as temporary editor of the *Aberdeen Saturday Pio-
       neer*, for which he writes articles and columns.

1891   Baum's fourth son, Kenneth, is born. Almost penniless,
       Baum moves to Chicago, where he becomes a reporter for
       the *Evening Post*.

1892   Unable to support his family on the scant wages of a re-
       porter, Baum also works as a traveling salesman for the chi-
       naware company Pitkin and Brooks.

1893   The enormous World's Columbian Exposition comes to
       Chicago. The United States experiences an economic de-
       pression.

1894   Rudyard Kipling's *The Jungle Book* is published.

1897   Baum's first children's story, *Mother Goose in Prose*, is pub-
       lished, with illustrations by Maxfield Parrish. Forced by ill
       health to give up selling, Baum founds *Show Window*, a
       journal on window trimming. The writer Opie Read intro-
       duces Baum to William Denslow, who will later illustrate
       books by Baum.

1899    *Father Goose, His Book*, with illustrations by Denslow, is published by George M. Hill company. Its success—it sells more copies than any other children's book this year—encourages Baum to continue writing. With extra money on hand, he buys a summerhouse in Macatawa Park, Michigan, that he names the Sign of the Goose.

1900    *The Wonderful Wizard of Oz*, with illustrations by Denslow, is published to resounding success. It has been in print ever since.

1901    *Dot and Tot of Merryland*, with illustrations by Denslow, is published.

1902    *The Wizard of Oz* is produced as a musical in Chicago and is sensationally popular. Baum splits with his illustrator William Denslow.

1903    The musical of *The Wizard of Oz* opens in New York. Baum tries to branch out by publishing the children's book *The Enchanted Island of Yew*, but it has little success.

1904    Responding to high demand for another Oz tale, Baum publishes a second novel, *The Marvelous Land of Oz*.

1905    *Queen Zixi of Ix* is published. Determined to write other kinds of works, Baum publishes an adult romance, *The Fate of a Crown*, under the pseudonym Schuyler Staunton.

1906    Baum publishes *Aunt Jane's Nieces*, the first of a series of ten novels written under the pen name Edith van Dyne.

1907    *Ozma of Oz* is published.

1908    Baum publishes *Dorothy and the Wizard of Oz*, in which he first calls himself the "Royal Historian of Oz." His *American Fairy Tales* appears.

1910    Baum tries to end the Oz series with *The Emerald City of Oz*. The Baum family moves to California. Struggling with poor health, Baum oversees the building of a house he calls Ozcot.

1911    *Peter and Wendy*, J. M. Barrie's *Peter Pan* play in novel form, is published.

1913    Because Baum's non-Oz books are not as successful as his Oz stories and he needs money, he writes *The Patchwork Girl of Oz*.

1914    Dreams of adapting his tales for film lead Baum to buy a movie production company; but it fails after producing a handful of films. World War I begins.

1918 Coronary illness and gallbladder surgery lead to a protracted period of bed rest. Despite his failing health, Baum continues to write.

1919 Baum has a heart attack on May 5, shortly after *The Magic of Oz* is published. He dies within twenty-four hours.

1920 Baum's final Oz story, *Glinda of Oz,* is published. Ruth Plumly Thompson takes over as "Royal Historian of Oz."

1939 MGM releases the classic film *The Wizard of Oz,* starring sixteen-year-old Judy Garland.

# The First American Children's Book

The first thing that you notice is what Dorothy notices: Kansas is gray.

> When Dorothy stood in the doorway and looked around, she could see nothing but the great gray prairie on every side. Not a tree nor a house broke the broad sweep of flat country that reached the edge of the sky in all directions. The sun had baked the plowed land into a gray mass, with little cracks running through it. Even the grass was not green, for the sun had burned the tops of the long blades until they were the same gray color to be seen everywhere. Once the house had been painted, but the sun blistered the paint and the rains washed it away, and now the house was as dull and gray as everything else (pp. 13–14).

Frank Baum was not the first to give Americans an American landscape in a children's book. Twain had done it in *The Adventures of Tom Sawyer* (1876) and even more radically in *Adventures of Huckleberry Finn* (1884), and Alcott had led out a suite of American preteens who grow into young adulthood with the March girls. But Twain and Alcott were writing juvenile books for a more mature audience. This book is Dorothy's, and Dorothy is a child, in her own words, "a helpless girl" and clearly if indefinably younger than any host of a child's narrative that Americans had encountered before 1900. We see Dorothy's world through Dorothy's eyes, a world constructed and policed, farmed and furnished by adults but modulated by a prose style that is childlike without being childish. In Dorothy, Baum gave America the first truly American *child* protagonist.[1]

Unlike the only two competing contemporary versions of preteen female protagonists, Lewis Carroll's Alice and J. M. Barrie's

Wendy (both ten-year-old girls), Baum put Dorothy in a book that features none of the potential cognitive difficulties that still tend to drive children (and some adults) away from the texts of *Alice in Wonderland* and *Peter Pan*. Though he admired *Alice in Wonderland* (1865), he also found it "rambling and incoherent," a judgment echoed by subsequent critics, and apparently refused Carroll's example of a highly internalized and ironic vision of a child's world.[2] The openings alone reveal the vast differences between these visions of childhood:

> Alice was beginning to get very tired of sitting by her sister on the bank, and of having nothing to do: once or twice she had peeped into the book her sister was reading, but it had no pictures or conversations in it, "and what is the use of a book," thought Alice, "without pictures or conversations?"
>
> So she was considering in her own mind, (as well as she could, for the hot day made her feel very sleepy and stupid,) whether the pleasure of making a daisy-chain would be worth the trouble of getting up and picking the daisies, when suddenly a white rabbit with pink eyes ran close by her.

There really is no "exterior" here because the author is taking advantage of the potential for exploiting a characteristic of children's narrative, the tendency to drift between literary and social space. It is all happening "in her own mind"—there are at least three such references in the opening paragraph—and in the syntactic environment, where the reader's attention is shunted like a Ping-Pong ball through bits of interior monologue ("and what is the use of a book," thought Alice, "without pictures or conversations?") and gates of parentheses, which suggest a mind that is capable of reflecting on itself, resulting in the severely hypotactic style we associate with high-octane Victorian satire, while the narrative elides interior and exterior and, by the third paragraph, is *in* Wonderland.

Baum also understood the central dilemma of any writer entering the genre—that children lend their name to the genre and nothing else—and dedicated himself to creating a thoroughly exteriorized vision of a child who finds herself in trouble. In that consists the decisive difference between Dorothy and her nearest

British and European counterparts. Alice's rabbit hole is not only a corridor to Wonderland but a passage into the unconscious; the result is a serially distorted view of a world she is not all that anxious to get back to as well as a mockery of ordered thought and behavior with no self-enunciating moral or logical center. Scholars love *Alice in Wonderland* because there is so much space for interpretive intervention; but scholarship, and Freud especially, has no place to stand in Oz and very little to say to Dorothy or about her journey. Oz is a lot of things—colorful, dangerous, silly—but no means as obsessively deranged or as "morally unintelligible" as Wonderland.[3] The world of *The Wonderful Wizard of Oz* is optimistic, not sarcastically aloof or, as it so often is in Barrie's *Peter Pan* (1904), archly satirical. Wonderland is a psychic, not a physical torment; Neverland is a theme park where the dominant modality is nostalgia. But Oz is a balloon ride away. MGM's decision to transform Dorothy into a trauma victim and Oz into a mental state blurs the essential difference between these two radically opposed visions of fairy tale and, possibly deliberately, turns Dorothy into an American Alice and a gracefully nuanced American romance into a psychological allegory. Given Hollywood's obsession with total cinematic disclosure and its prime directive that no fact must ever go unexplained, you get the 1939 film—a work of genius, but not of Baum's genius.[4]

So for readers who come to the novel after having grown up with the movie, the biggest shock is to find in the novel none of the film's comforting, gap-filling backstory. Some of the cinematic revisions, such as the snowstorm that wakes the sleepers in the poppy field and that replaces their rescue by the Queen of the Mice in chapter IX, were cost-efficient alternatives to special effects that might have proven impossible or inadequate to the illusion.[5] The change from Silver Shoes to Ruby Slippers in the 1939 movie, as most people know, was dictated by technical considerations (red showed up more vividly on the film stock of the period than silver); and American culture would be poorer without some of its memorable dialogue. But the principal changes are in the overall characterization and in retrospect seem less defensible. In the book Uncle Henry and Auntie Em never really emerge from the background and appear together only in chapter I, Auntie Em appearing alone in the very brief closing chapter. The film, however, shows them as loveable (if two-toned) representatives of a loveable Kansas home. Margaret Hamilton's Wicked Witch turns out to be one more ripple in Dorothy's concussed subconscious and the Kansas prototype of the Wicked Witch of the West, who even has a *name*—Almira Gulch. Auntie Em is hardly the "thin and gaunt," childless old woman whose eyes had lost their sparkle and were as gray as Kansas. She is an all-American original with a tongue and a personality to match. "Almira Gulch," she says on hearing of Almira's plan to destroy Toto, "just because you own half the county doesn't mean you have the power to run the rest of us!" Perhaps the biggest change is in Dorothy herself, who is actually a feistier child in the novel than on film. Consider the witch's death. The film stages the event as an accident—Dorothy aims a bucket of water at the burning Scarecrow and douses the witch instead. But the novel makes it no accident. The witch tricks Dorothy and obtains one of her Silver Shoes. Dorothy gets "so very angry that she picked up the bucket of water that stood near and dashed it over the Witch." Judy Garland's Dorothy is tearfully apologetic; Baum's is outspoken and "angry."[6]

The screenwriters (Noel Langley, Florence Ryerson, and Edgar Allan Woolf) also expanded the roles of the three companions and turned the Scarecrow, Tin Woodman, and Lion into metamorphosed versions of farmhands named Hunk, Hickory, and Zeke. Professor Marvel (Frank Morgan), the genial fraud who watches Dorothy head off as the tornado prepares to descend, reenters her dream vision as the Wizard (as well as, once in the City of Oz, the doorman of the Emerald City, a cabdriver, and the Wizard's guard). These were more than touches of simple psychological realism. Like the technical stroke to shift to color from black and white when Dorothy arrives in Munchkin Land and the suddenly indispensable musical score, these permanent contributions to the Oz mythology are also improvisations that may not necessarily constitute improvements.[7] They blur the clarity of the original, superimposing a second relational network on a clearer original. Dorothy and her companions each lack something and venture to the Emerald City to request it of the Wizard to find it, but in the novel neither the companions nor their deficiencies have reciprocal counterparts in the "real" world of Kansas. Oz is no Purgatory or compensatory educational experience, and it is definitely no metaphor for unconsciousness. Yet the film persuades the audience of a nearly allegorical symmetry between Kansas and Oz and raises unique questions. Is this Dorothy's way of disclosing in dream truths too dangerous or painful to bear while awake? Are the three companions, like the three beasts who temporarily block Dante's entrance to Hell, reflections of flaws in her personality? We don't really know. The movie supplies teasing closures to questions that only it raises. The screenwriters' brilliant adaptation—whether you find it welcome or not—turns each character into a symbolic referent, a point on a carefully plotted postcyclonic rainbow that begins and ends in Kansas. As a result, the film displaces emphasis from fantasy to psychology and makes several "unforgivable" changes.[8] Whatever its justification in commercial or technical terms, the film forces its audience to measure the distance between Kansas and Oz in psychic, not imaginative, terms; it tidies up certain loose ends, such as the origins of the Tin Woodman and the Scarecrow, each of whose histories is explained in the book, by eliminating the need for explanations. Everything that occurs in the end occurs in Dorothy's mind.

This is an essential point: Baum's Oz, like the Elysian Fields in Greek mythology or the witch's house in "Hansel and Gretel," is a place you can get to from here. There is no complicated prospectus, more fit for adults than children, of dream projections of waking originals. The text has a serene confidence in its own imaginative conditions that, along with its disquietingly simple style, are its lasting strengths. For those raised on the movie, what is "missing" is surface complexity, density of characterization, and witty dialogue. Baum's prose is clear and childlike and represents an uncompromising attention to plot rather than style, to events over character. It's almost as if children's literature had found in Baum its own Homer, a writer whose straightforward and occasionally pedestrian style is the determined outcome of the oddness of the story he has to tell. You may miss the character overlays of the film and its calculated verbal ironies, derivative of the more sophisticated children's books. You may long for the *closure* you feel when you see Ray Bolger behind the Scarecrow's outlines or hear the Wizard in Professor Marvel's voice.[9] On the other hand, the novel dispensed with *Wonderland*-ish exits such as Dorothy's coming to at the end or the final tableau where the ensemble, including Professor Marvel, gathers around her bed like a Broadway cast taking a second bow. While the last person to consult in matters of intention is the author, it's noteworthy that Baum's stated purpose was to "please children of today" with "a modernized fairy tale, in which the wonderment and joy are retained and the heartaches and nightmares are left out" (p. 3). Simplicity, in other words, was his goal, not stylistic flash or psychological nuance.

For students of popular literature, one of the least appealing features of *The Wonderful Wizard of Oz* and its thirteen sequels may be its flat-affect style and its drifting meanings. *Alice in Wonderland* has been the subject of dissertations and a Norton Critical Edition.[10] Barrie's *Peter Pan*, not yet a Norton, was the subject of a famous and still-resonant critical attack; and Barrie, like Carroll/Dodgson, is still a person of intense biographical interest, much of it directed at his suspiciously homoerotic attachment to the Davies boys.[11] Andersen and the Brothers Grimm have attracted as many footnotes as readers. By contrast *The Wizard of Oz*, always clear sailing for children, is the horse latitudes for scholars, with its author's intentions having drained away into the simple medium of his narrative and its oddities petrified into a system of connections that, as Edith Hamilton remarked of Greek myth, is comprehensive but never coherent. Its very simplicity, in fact, has paradoxically been a barrier to using it in education.[12] Yet Dorothy's book remains nonetheless a book Dorothy herself would likely have been able to read—and probably on her own. Generations of readers struggle with Andersen's moral inflexibility and his tendency to punish his female protagonists; they find the Grimm's Fairy Tales as annoyingly elliptical as they find Andersen overwrought; and in both notice a fascination with acts of cruelty and violence. *Alice in Wonderland*, though not violent, is an intensely linguistic construct of wacky wordplay, allusion, and parody that features but really does not include the child. Wendy, like Alice, is ten, but what ten-year-old will understand what *Peter Pan*'s obnoxious narrator is alluding to when he compares Captain Hook to "the Sea-Cook"—or Long John Silver of *Treasure Island*? To get an allusion one must have read as much as the author. The allusive range of any text—whether a children's book or Eliot's *The Waste*

*Land*—is an unspoken measure and reflection of the author's education and the core curriculum of cultural expectations and values that inform it. More than one reader has asked himself—or his parents— whether protagonists like Alice or Wendy would be able to read the books they are in. Who asks that question about *The Wonderful Wizard of Oz*?

The difficulty is not always cognitive. The emotional weather in Andersen, Carroll, and Barrie can be dark, wild, and off-putting. Irony is a cognitive threshold for all readers; for children it can be disabling or off-limits. (Try being sarcastic with even the brightest of five-year-olds and he or she may never forgive you.) Irony is a kind of negative exemplification, where you listen to one thing and hear it twice; it is as though the text were singing in harmony with its own implications. Most of life for most children must come with a script, but irony assumes that you already have one; and in fairy tales, which have traditionally been children's earliest scripted plays, the irony is either structural or nonexistent. But when the Little Mermaid's grandmother tells her that the only way that she can gain a human soul would be for the prince "to love you so much that you were more to him than his father or mother," only those who get the allusion to the marriage ceremony will appreciate the bittersweet irony. Tinker Bell's mantraic response of "silly ass" in response to Peter's repeated failure to see that her feelings for him are romantic may inspire a ten-year-old's smile but probably not her recognition. For better or worse, confusion like this never troubles readers of the Oz books, where the prevailing emotional weather is optimistic and the tonalities nearly irony free.

Nearly, but not completely. Frank Baum, who was crazy about puns, filled the book with soft-pedaled double entendres—which, for many of us, is Irony 101. Removing the Scarecrow's head in chapter XVI, the Wizard empties the straw and fills the head "with a measure of bran, which he mixed with a great many pins and needles," and then announces, "Hereafter you will be a great man, for I have given you a lot of bran-new brains" (p. 160). A moment later the Lion says of the pins and needles, "That is proof that he is sharp" (p. 160). Comparing the Tin Woodman to the Scarecrow, Glinda says to the former, "You are really brighter than he is— when you are well polished" (p. 208). Some of Baum's puns are subtler, but not by much, such as the Tin Woodman's declaration in chapter XV that he will "bear all [his] unhappiness without a murmur" (p. 155), which is exactly what you would expect of a character with no heartbeat. Other wordplays are contextual: If you were to ask the brainless Scarecrow the question usually posed to fools—"Were you born yesterday?"—he would have to say yes, because, as he relates in chapter III, he actually *was* born yesterday.

Baum's novel is also a staging area for a form of childproof character irony called the irony of self-betrayal, a dramatic or situational irony that is both childproof and child safe.[13] The obvious example is the brainless Scarecrow's habit of coming up with good ideas. It is he who proposes (in chapter VII, p. 68) the order in which the friends must leap the first chasm, each mounted on the Lion's back. When the Lion asks, "Who will go first?" the Scarecrow explains his reply—"I will"—in splendidly rational terms: "If you found that you could not jump over the gulf, Dorothy would be killed, or the Tin Woodman badly dented on the rocks below. But if I am on your back it will not matter so much, for the fall would not hurt me at all." Moments later, after directing the Tin Woodman to chop down a tree in order to make a bridge across the second chasm so they can escape the pursuing Kalidahs, the Lion remarks, "One would almost suspect you had brains in your head, instead of straw" (p. 70). Immediately afterward, the Scarecrow again figures out how to send the marauding Kalidahs crashing into the gulf (p. 70) and asks the Queen of the field mice to enlist the aid of her subjects in dragging the Lion from the poppy field (p. 87).

One of the funniest sites for self-contradiction is the heartless Tin Woodman, who is constantly bursting into "tears of sorrow and regret" over this or that violation of the natural order, such as his accidental squashing of a beetle in chapter VI:

> "This will serve me a lesson," said he, "to look where I step. For if I should kill another bug or beetle I should surely cry again, and crying rusts my jaw so that I cannot speak."
>
> Thereafter he walked very carefully, with his eyes on the road, and when he saw a tiny ant toiling by he would step over it, so as not to harm it. The Tin Woodman knew very well he had no heart, and therefore he took great care never to be cruel or unkind to anything.

"You people with hearts," he said, "have something to guide you, and need never do wrong; but I have no heart, and so I must be very careful" (pp. 63–64).

The contradictions pile up: The brainless come up with the brainiest ideas, the heartless are supersensitive, and the cowardly admit, courageously, to being a coward (and then perform feats of physical daring). The fact that the absence of a heart actually produces something more profound—intense regard for everything that moves—is completely lost on the Woodman, just as the Scarecrow is clueless when it comes to knowing the real meaning of having brains. All three companions are alike in assuming a transparent relationship between signs and their meanings—brains, heart, and courage—and this, of course, is the book's running joke: All three already possess what they go looking for. Sheldon Cashdan has supplied probably the best short description of the novel in noting how it "focuses on perceived shortcoming in the self as opposed to excesses."[14] The operative word there is *perceived*. The thematic center of *The Wonderful Wizard of Oz*, like that of any discovery narrative or rite of passage, is a simple message: Accept yourself for what you are.

## II

The differences between Dorothy and her overseas cousins aside, her story, like Wendy's and Alice's, is a version of the heroic quest, from Gilgamesh through Odysseus and Aeneas to Huck Finn, Gully Foyle (the protagonist of Alfred Bester's science-fiction novel *The Stars My Destination*), and Luke Skywalker.[15] *The Wizard of Oz* is an odyssey redacted for children and an elaboration of microquests like "Hansel and Gretel" and "The Little Mermaid." Perry Nodelman has described these as "home-away-home" stories, child-sized versions of Northrop Frye's Monomyth.[16] It is the same story that Western culture has in general outline been telling itself for millennia: Self-knowledge requires physical and emotional self-testing, heroes are often reluctant to answer the call, and at the center of the journey is an encounter with profound truths that connect us with our pasts. In more senses than one, Dorothy's adventure fits the description, from her accidental landing in Oz to her reluctant acceptance of her power to her recognition, standing in the Wizard's hall, that not even the lovely Emerald City of Oz can top gray Kansas. Baum's story is a child's meditation on Homer's second great theme, *nostalgia*, and, like Odysseus, whose name means "born for trouble," his protagonist has a last name (Gale) that is a subtle predictor of the event, a tornadic windstorm, that determines her destiny.[17] Alison Lurie has pointed out how women tend to occupy the dominant roles in all the Oz books, another of its similarities, accidental or not, to Homer's *Odyssey*, also dominated by women and traditionally called our great domestic epic.[18]

While the imaginative world of Oz bears a family resemblance to whole libraries of fantasy and adventure, it is hard to identify Baum's principal influences. He so artfully sublimates his sources they seem sui generis, reminders of Eliot's remark that bad writers borrow and good writers steal. Some, like the kind Stork, are elements that appear in all children's literature, which features lots of talking animals—the noteworthy exception being Toto, who exemplifies that conundrum of children's literature, the Goofy/Pluto Quandary—that is, why some animals speak and others do not, why Goofy has full command of the language and Pluto, Mickey's dog, can only bark.[19] Some elements of suggestive iconographic value, such as the Wicked Witch's dread of water or the fact that her blood has all dried up, seem easily parsed. Others are less certain. The mark on Dorothy's forehead left by the Good Witch of the North is talismanic, like Achilles' unprotected heel or the more contemporary inheritor of the same idea, the lightning-bolt scar on Harry Potter's brow. Does it also point to the mark made by offended deity to protect Cain from harm and to perpetuate his torment? When Odysseus visits Hell in book 11 of the *Odyssey*, the reason is to get directions home from Tiresias, and, similarly, Dorothy undertakes the trip to the Emerald City to ask the Wizard how to get back to Kansas. Yet Oz is no more Hades than Hades Oz. The bar of iron that the Witch places in the middle of her kitchen floor to trip up Dorothy half works—Dorothy trips and loses one of her Silver Shoes—but also inverts tradition: Bar iron is usually associated with warding off demons, not innocent little girls. The witch has a single cyclopean eye that announces a disturbing union of monstrosity and omniscience (and to some may point to Freemasonry's single eye that appears on U.S. currency). In Greek myth, Hermes wears a cap of wings, and in Baum's Oz Dorothy has a Golden Cap. The Winged Monkeys seem related to neutral instrumentalities of evil authority like the Harpies or Wagner's Valkyrie, but neither of these antecedents is as reasonable or eloquent as Baum's equivalents.[20] The apportionment of real estate in Oz is impressive, with the witches governing regions designated by the four cardinal points. But why did Baum assign positive moral values to north and south and negative to east and west—a literary fact, or accident, that Littlefield would use sixty-four years later when he advanced his famous reading of the book as a political allegory?[21]

Or, again, take those Silver Shoes. They seem to reach back to the Cinderella story but in a not entirely helpful way. Dorothy is not Cinderella—and not only because she is of less than marrying age. Dorothy's home life is comfortable and happy; moreover, all Cinderellas, male or female, are sponsored by some natural agency that functions as a parent surrogate—a fairy godmother, a Mother Holle, the spectral grandmother of the Little Match Girl, or in derivatives like *Flashdance* or *Rocky*, as the protagonist's aging female dance instructor or his grouchy fight trainer. Every Cinderella is special in the first place, a member of a natural aristocracy who has gone unrecognized by dog-and-cat humanity until Nature intervenes and teaches the world to see beauty with Nature's eyes. This is children's literature's own law of natural selection, which states that no naturally gifted child must ever be forced to suffer for very long either social exploitation, social invisibility, or familial marginality. The Cinderella scenario hardly applies to Dorothy, who is special only *after* she is picked up and set down in Oz. She has a happy home, is only technically "homeless" while in Oz, and has two adoptive parents who love her. She is, moreover, a typical little girl from Kansas whose most precious gift is that she knows it. Her confinement in the castle of the Wicked Witch seems an analogue to Cinderella's situation, but Dorothy does little work and spends part of her time in bitter tears. Each invocation of possible precedent only introduces more alienating distance. Scattered throughout the novel there are many such symbols that seem interpretive dead ends—the fact that white is the witch color, for instance, which inverts the anticipated hierarchy of color-coded values, or that, as we learn in chapter XII, the witch is afraid of the dark. The same is true of so many story elements that their appearances, rather than being iterations of some ancient property of fantastic literature, are really opportunities for Baum to empty them and then fill them with his own American content. Whence the continuing and probably endless parade of allegorical readings of the novel, from Henry Littlefield's to Herblock's famous 1939 cartoon, in which Hitler is cast as the Wicked Witch of the West and Mussolini one of the Flying Monkeys. Baum approached his sources like someone on a shopping spree rather than one conducting a calculated raid.

Perhaps this whimsicality also explains why certain apparently pregnant details lead nowhere, such as the man in the small house Dorothy and her companions stop at on the way to the Emerald City, who "had hurt his leg, and was lying on the couch in a corner" (pp. 94–95), the "seven passages and three flights of steps" (pp.104–105) through which Dorothy is led on the way to her room in the Palace, or the fact that the Wizard charges them to come to his Throne Room "at four minutes after nine o'clock" in the morning (p. 148). Was Baum preparing some role for the character with the bad leg that he either forgot about or failed to find a place for? Was one of his children, perhaps, born at 9:04 A.M.? Or are these details simply forgivable inconsistencies, like the behavior of the Tin Woodman, who is moved to tears when he accidentally steps on a bug yet slays a wildcat and forty wolves, or that Dorothy is suddenly found to be wearing a whistle "that she had always carried about her neck since the Queen of the Mice had given it to her" (p. 140), when, in fact, this never happened?

Baum's use of colors is particularly intriguing. There were initially four witches, and by the end of chapter III only one bad one, the Witch of the West, is left. (Should we make anything of the fact that by her very arrival in Oz Dorothy instantly tips the balance in favor of the good and dresses in a frock of white, the witch color, and blue?) Green, the color of the Emerald City, has a persistently ambiguous value in literature, a two-headed semantic arrow that points in opposite or divergent directions. While it gestures to nature and to the appealing presence of natural forces, like nature itself it can possess a malign, counter-Wordsworthian aspect. In *Gawain and the Green Knight,* for instance, green is assigned to a figure who mingles both beauty and monstrosity, virtue and cruelty; in *The Great Gatsby*, green is the color of the inspirational light at the end of Daisy Buchanan's dock and of the "death car" that kills Myrtle Wilson. But what does Baum's selection of green represent?[22] The same is true of blue, the Munchkin's "favorite" color and the one "most frequently seen," according to Biedermann, "as a symbol for things of the spirit and the intellect"—from the Virgin Mary's mantle in stained glass windows to Veronica Sawyer's outfits in Michael Lehmann's *Heathers* (1989).[23] Does Dorothy's progression from a blue-dominated land to a "green" destination make some significant commentary on her journey, or is the relationship an accidental correlation? Leading the inexplicables is the name *Oz* itself.[24] Baum, who as Hearn says was not the most careful writer, clearly had fun with his material—extemporizing from sources that may in the long run have been purely and hopelessly autobiographical.

Unlike the Freudian dimensions that Alice finds at the bottom of the rabbit hole, all the dangers in Oz are external. And a general understanding prevails. When the Wicked Witch dispatches the Winged Monkeys she instructs them to destroy all except the Lion ("I have a mind to harness him like a horse, and make him work") (p. 122), they successfully carry out her orders until they reach Dorothy:

> The leader of the Winged Monkeys flew up to her, his long, hairy arms stretched out and his ugly face grinning terribly; but he saw the mark of the good Witch's kiss upon her forehead and stopped short, motioning the others not to touch her.
>
> "We dare not harm this little girl," he said to them, "for she is protected by the Power of Good, and that is greater than the Power of Evil" (p. 123).

In Oz, and nearly everywhere in fantasy, this is the prime directive: Good is inevitably stronger than evil. It informs Dorothy's appeal to the Wizard and, prior to that, the behavior of the Stork, and it is one more reason, arguably the principal one, for the discomfort experienced by the first generation of fans of the book who were faced with a troubling ambiguity. Oz is a place where good dominates, but where you will also find that impossible contradiction, the good witch. This is by all evidence Frank Baum's invention and arguably his lasting contribution to the representational vocabulary of Western literature. Nowhere do you find a good witch before Baum, who combines a traditional occult figure with the American progressive's optimistic faith in human nature—what is nowadays termed, often disparagingly, secular humanism—and invents a whole new moral typology. The righteous who may be tempted to read J. K. Rowling understand the dilemma intimately. What good is it if the message is consonant with Christian morality but the vehicle is not? In the long run, Baum's entrepreneurial approach to tradition echoed Whitman's cry of "creeds and schools in abeyance"; like Whitman, Baum wanted to give America something completely new—the concept of "neutral magic," of the occult as something rationally available and subject to domestication without the help of traditionally "demonic" assistants. The outcome is everywhere around us, in films especially, from the Force in *Star Wars* to *Practical Magic*. Baum's morality is rooted in humanistic ideals and only incidentally in scriptural principles.

Adding to the appeal of *The Wonderful Wizard of Oz* was the fact that its protagonist shared many of the audience's prejudices. Dorothy, a product of the core curriculum of American morality, reacts the way a reader in 1900 would have reacted. "I thought all witches were wicked," she says forcefully to the Good Witch of the North in chapter II. The witch's reply, which includes a lesson in Oz geography keyed to which witch owns what, does little to assuage her:

"But," said Dorothy, after a moment's thought, "Aunt Em has told me that the witches were all dead—years and years ago."

"Who is Aunt Em?" inquired the little old woman.

"She is my aunt who lives in Kansas, where I came from."

The Witch of the North seemed to think for a time, with her head bowed and her eyes upon the ground. Then she looked up and said,

"I do not know where Kansas is, for I have never heard that country mentioned before. But tell me, is it a civilized country?"

"Oh, yes;" replied Dorothy.

"Then that accounts for it. In the civilized countries I believe
there are no witches left; nor wizards, nor sorceresses, nor magicians. But, you see, the Land of Oz has never been civilized, for we
are cut off from all the rest of the world. Therefore we still have
witches and wizards amongst us" (p. 25).

This exchange has essential premonitory value. Many in the audience who believed as Dorothy did ("all witches [are] wicked")
might have objected to the whole concept of a Good Witch, one
certainly without scriptural or moral precedent. The only witches
who appear in the Bible came to their power through satanic influence; prior to that the only appeal is to Greek myth's two isolated
examples, Circe and Medea, either of whom occupy a different reg-
ister since, technically, neither had any traffic with the infernal. As
for fairy tales, which by then had been circulating at least since
Grimms' tales appeared in English in 1826, they feature neither
"good" witches nor exemplary human practitioners of the black
arts.[25] Yet Baum gives his audience a strange, tricky place to stand
in Dorothy's narrative by having Dorothy ask *their* question and receive an answer that, couched in the suggestion that Kansas is a
synechdoche for civilization, must have struck an ambivalent
chord. His essential imaginative discovery was that to be a witch did
not mean you belonged to some dark aristocracy of the spirit because magic was an instrumentality like electricity, magnetism, or
fire.[26] In this new republic of the imagination, a person could become a president, a wizard, a person with brains, or a witch.

In the longest run, Baum's book is remarkable for its Emerson-
ian attitude toward science, the future, and technology. Everywhere you look in *The Wonderful Wizard of Oz* you find gadgets or
inventions that seem to reflect the adventurousness of its author's
imagination. The Wizard of Oz, hardly a bad man after all (and
certainly no wizard), is originally from Omaha and arrives (and de-
parts) by balloon. His transformation of Oz into the Emerald City,
a green utopia, is accomplished mostly by salesmanship—he dis-
tributes among the population green spectacles—and thereby joins

that distinguished cast of commercial foot soldiers in American literature, from Stephen Crane's drummer in "The Bride Comes to
Yellow Sky" through Dreiser's Hurstwood (in *Sister Carrie*), Fitzger-
ald's Nick Carraway all the way up (or down) to Willy Loman. The
Wizard of Oz produces "wonders" by means of technical daring or
simple chicanery, a stark contrast to the victories of the witches,
both good and bad, who surround (and fear) him; the Emerald City
of Oz is the elision of convention and novelty, of the typical magical props of fantasy with nuts-and-bolts American technology. The
magical Silver Shoes coexist with the Wizard's balloon, the balloon
with the Wicked Witch, the tinkers and the tinsmiths with the
Winged Monkeys and that oddest of Oz's brain belches, the dainty
china people. The title of chapter XVI, "The Magic Art of the
Great Humbug," effectively summarizes what Baum is up to: forg-
ing an alliance between the human and the occult, the latter being
owned by the former. Under no compulsion to separate the fantastic from the science fiction element, he ignores the self-consciously
generic distinction, still enforced on newsstands where you can
find *Analog* side by side with *The Magazine of Fantasy and Science
Fiction*, between the magical and the manufactured. With Oz he
designed an alternative Wonderland—American, external, and ac-
cessible.

And a wizard, lest we forget, whose success—to the extent we
credit it as such—is the result not of black magic but benign chicanery and fairground illusion. It's always amazed me how we tend
to overlook the fact that the title is as ironic as *The Great Gatsby*.
Baum's Wizard is to the traditional sorcerer what Yossarian is to the
hero—a comic, and therefore unconventional representative of a
class of characters whom we rarely, if ever, laugh at when we see
them. He is an antiwizard, a disarmingly likable fraud who has
everybody in town wearing green spectacles and who builds a balloon, that last word in air travel in Baum's day, but forgets to rig it
with controls—his balloon will only descend, it appears, when the
hot air cools. The point is not that Frank Baum considered all wizards frauds—which would be equivalent to suggesting that he had
made up his mind about the nature of all fantasy—but that he
could imagine a fraud who might, given the right opportunity, turn
out to be a pretty good wizard. Moral categories in Oz are identified

by *how* you use what you have and not by your innate character traits—which once upon a time was what America stood for. Oz, in other words, is no aristocracy but a magical democracy. You can be anything you want—wizard or witch—without worrying that your choices are front-loaded by a particular set of values. For some, the appeal of fantasies like Andersen's and Grimms', continuing through Carroll and directly into Rowling, is a lingering nostalgia for an aristocracy of moral personality, where distinctions are innate and a person is born, as Blake said, "a garden ready and planted." Into those fantasies enter characters who bridge the gaps and introduce welcome elements of ambiguity. Even Harry Potter, that idealization of the adolescent consumer, has an elite pedigree that separates him from the Mudbloods. But Dorothy is hardly an aristocrat, and the Oz she enters is ambiguous from the beginning, a triumph of coexistent and codependent moral and imaginative technologies. One is the ancient one of fairy tale and fantastic literature, of wicked witches with nonaligned helpers, natural agents that serve as liminal figures, talking animals and enchanted footwear. The other is Baum's, whose sublimest invention is this place where the extraordinary and the everyday live side by side and mirror each other. When the good witch says that Oz is "more powerful" than any of the other witches in Oz, she is preparing the reader for the book's gentlest but most engaging irony. "How can I help being a humbug," he says after he is exposed, "when all these people make me do things that everybody knows can't be done?" (pp. 162–163). But, of course, they *don't* know. The Wizard of Oz's power is ultimately dependent on the gullibility of his audience and his sense of supply and demand. At bottom he may not be much of a wizard, as he himself admits. But he is still a pretty good American salesman. And in Oz, salesmanship—that improbably American contribution to Western cultural values—is stronger than sorcery.

---

**J. T. Barbarese,** an authority on children's literature, teaches at Rutgers University in Camden, New Jersey, where he is a member of the Rutgers Center for Children and Childhood Studies. He is the author of four books of poetry and a translation of Euripides. His fourth volume of poetry, *The Black Beach* (University of North

Texas Press), was awarded the Vassar Miller Prize for poetry in 2004. He is also the author of *New Science* (University of Georgia Press, 1989) and *A Very Small World* (Orchises Press, 2004). His poems have appeared in *Atlantic Monthly, Boulevard, Georgia Review, Denver Quarterly, Sewanee Review,* and *Poetry,* and most recently in the anthology *The Italian-American Reader* (Morrow, 2003). His short fiction has appeared in *Story Quarterly* and *North American Review,* and his critical essays and literary journalism have appeared in a variety of publications, from *Tri-Quarterly, Studies in English Literature, The Looking Glass,* and the *Journal of Modern Literature* to the *Georgia Review* and the *New York Times.* He is presently working on a collection of essays on Little League baseball in America.

## Notes

1. Michael Patrick Hearn reports that Dorothy "may have been no more than five or six years old when [she] took her first trip to Oz," which he calculates based on material in the sequels, on Denslow's drawings, and on a remark made by one of Baum's sons that Baum "wrote the book for children two to six years old." See Hearn, *The Annotated Wonderful Wizard of Oz,* 2000, p. 35, note 4. See "For Further Reading."

2. Baum, quoted in Hearn, p. 12, note 1.

3. Donald Rackin, "Blessed Rage," in Lewis Carroll, *Alice in Wonderland,* edited by Donald J. Gray, A Norton Critical Edition, second edition, New York: W. W. Norton, 1971, p. 401.

4. Mark Evan Swartz, author of *Oz Before the Rainbow,* chronicles the evolution of adaptations of *The Wizard of Oz* and demonstrates the inaccuracy of blaming MGM and Victor Fleming for all these changes. As early as the 1910 one-reel silent version of the novel, which itself inherited elements from the 1902 stage version, filmmakers, some of them with Baum's blessing, had begun blurring the line between Kansas and Oz. One way to look at the 1939 film

adaptation is that it was a vast improvement on changes already introduced in earlier adaptations and raised several stop-gaps and audience concessions to the level of high art.

5. The snowstorm was introduced in the 1902 musical and may have been Baum's own suggestion. See Hearn, p. 156, note 5.

6. Hearn reports that elementary schools occasionally put Dorothy on trial for murder. See Hearn, p. 226, note 18.

7. The idea to shifting from sepia to Technicolor when Dorothy steps out of the house was, as it turns out, a duplication of an effect produced in an earlier, shorter 1933 cartoon version that received limited distribution. See Hearn, p. 33, note 2.

8. Hearn, p. 27, note 13.

9. The idea of a play that tacitly embodies its interpretation did not begin or end with *The Wizard of Oz*. The staging of *Peter Pan* routinely casts the same actor to play both Mr. Darling and Captain Hook, and legend has it that in Sophocles' *Philoctetes* the same actor played the role of both the evil Odysseus and the god Heracles, who arrives as a deus ex machina.

10. Though there have been dissertations written on *The Wonderful Wizard of Oz*, it has tended to attract a good deal less scholarly interest because on the surface it offers scholarship too little opportunity to do what it does best—quibble.

11. Jacqueline Rose, *The Case of* Peter Pan, *or, the Impossibility of Children's Fiction*, London: Macmillan, 1984. Both Dodgson and Barrie are the subject of biopics. In the case of Barrie, the most recent is *Finding Neverland* (2004).

12. The reception history of *The Wonderful Wizard of Oz* includes an outburst of hostility around the centennial of Baum's birth in 1956, when teachers who found the book badly written and useless in the classroom organized a protest against it. Martin Gardner and Russel B. Nye's book, *The Wizard of Oz & Who He Was*, was an attempt to

redress the charges that the book was pedagogically unsound and refute the attacks on Baum's admittedly thin style.

13. The term was coined by D. C. Muecke. See *Irony*, edited by J. D. Jump. London: Metheun, 1970.

14. Sheldon Cashdan, *The Witch Must Die: How Fairy Tales Shape Our Lives*, New York: Basic Books, 1999, p. 218.

15. George Lucas has openly admitted the influence of the characters in *The Wizard of Oz* on his own foursome of Luke, Princess Leia, Han Solo, and Chewbaca.

16. See Joseph Campbell, *The Hero with a Thousand Faces*, Princeton, NJ: Princeton University Press, 1968, p. 114. See also Northrop Frye, *The Anatomy of Criticism: Four Essays*, Princeton, NJ: Princeton University Press, 2000, and Perry Nodelman, *The Pleasures of Children's Literature*, New York: Longman, 1992, for discussions and applications of the archetypal approach. For Jung's presentation of archetype, see *Symbols of Transformation*, second edition, translated by R. F. C. Hull, Princeton, NJ: Princeton University Press, 1967. Hearn notes that Campbell never mentions *The Wizard of Oz* and then proceeds to demonstrate how consistent it is with Campbell's heuristic. See Hearn, p. 59, note 5.

17. Other examples are Moses (*moishe*, "to pull out," an allusion to his being placed in a basket of reeds) and Oedipus ("swollen foot"). Dorothy's last name is revealed in the third novel in the series, *Ozma of Oz* (1907) but actually makes its first appearance in the 1902 musical as a punning reference to how she got to Oz and may have been supplied by the director. See Hearn, p. 48, note 30.

18. Alison Lurie, "The Oddness of Oz," *The New York Review of Books*, December 21, 2000, pp. 16–24.

19. This may seem absurdly unimportant to adults but is of some interest to attentive children. Hearn reports that in a later Oz book it is revealed that Toto could talk all along, but he chose not to.

20. In the MGM version of 1939, the leader of the Winged Monkeys is played by actor Pat Walshe and has a name (Nikko), several lines, and billing.

21. Baum's witches, as I discuss later, are among his greatest inventions. They are related to traditional witches only insofar as they use magic. Their power is not "demonic" in origin—at least not technically.

22. According to Hearn, "the change from one region to another follows the principles of color theory." Hearn, p. 61, note 7.

23. Hans Biedermann, *Dictionary of Symbolism*, translated by James Hulbert, New York: Meridian, 1994), p. 158. According to G. Heinz Mohr (whose *Lexikon der Symbole*, Düsseldorf und Köln: Diederichs, 1981, is referenced in Biedermann), "Christian symbolism finds green 'equidistant from the blue of heaven, the red of hell . . . an intermediate and mediating color, soothing, refreshing, human, a color of contemplation, of the expectation of resurrection" (Biedermann, p. 158). Color analysis based on traditional value assignments, moreover, would have to explain why it is that Glinda's holdings, the Land of the Quadlings, is marked in red on the map of Oz that Baum created and that the Wicked Witch controlled the Winkie Country, which is colored yellow.

24. The name came as either an afterthought or an accident. "One evening while telling his children and their friends a story about a little girl named Dorothy who was carried off by a cyclone to a fairyland, Baum was asked what was the name of the strange country. Looking about the room, his eye fell upon the drawers of the filing cabinet, which were labeled 'A–N' and 'O–Z'; he told the children it was the Land of Oz." See Hearn, p. 43, note 17, for this and other ingenious explanations.

25. The old woman named Mother Holle in the Grimm's fairy tale of the same name, for instance, is a figuration of Mother Nature and is clearly super- or inhuman, unlike, by way of contrast, the witch who attempts to eat Hansel and Gretel. Mother Holle is, in fact, a type not of the Good Witch but of embodiments of providence or

natural order, which is inevitably, and aggressively, good in children's literature.

26. Baum's *The Master Key: An Electrical Fairy Tale* (1901) a boy named Rob discovers the power of electricity when he summons accidentally the Demon of Electricity. The demon, not incidentally, is another of Baum's crossbred characterizations who informs Rob that "demons may be either good or bad, like any other class of beings. Originally all demons were good, yet of late years people have come to consider all demons evil." The demon then cites a passage from Hesiod, which is interesting in that the root of *demon* is the ancient Greek word *daimon* which means "spirit" or "deity."

# Introduction

Folklore, legends, myths and fairy tales have followed childhood through the ages, for every healthy youngster has a wholesome and instinctive love for stories fantastic, marvelous and manifestly unreal. The winged fairies of Grimm and Andersen have brought more happiness to childish hearts than all other human creations.

Yet the old-time fairy tale, having served for generations, may now be classed as "historical" in the children's library; for the time has come for a series of newer "wonder tales" in which the stereotyped genie, dwarf and fairy are eliminated, together with all the horrible and blood-curdling incidents devised by their authors to point a fearsome moral to each tale. Modern education includes morality; therefore the modern child seeks only entertainment in its wonder-tales and gladly dispenses with all disagreeable incidents.

Having this thought in mind, the story of "The Wonderful Wizard of Oz" was written solely to please children of today. It aspires to being a modernized fairy tale, in which the wonderment and joy are retained and the heartaches and nightmares are left out.

L. FRANK BAUM
*Chicago, April, 1900*

# THE WONDERFUL
# WIZARD OF OZ

# LIST OF CHAPTERS

I   The Cyclone   11

II   The Council with The Munchkins   19

III   How Dorothy Saved the Scarecrow   29

IV   The Road Through the Forest   39

V   The Rescue of the Tin Woodman   47

VI   The Cowardly Lion   57

VII   The Journey to The Great Oz   65

VIII   The Deadly Poppy Field   73

IX   The Queen of the Field Mice   83

X   The Guardian of the Gates   91

XI   The Wonderful Emerald City of Oz   101

XII   The Search for the Wicked Witch   115

XIII   The Rescue   129

XIV   The Winged Monkeys   137

XV   The Discovery of Oz, The Terrible   145

XVI   The Magic Art of the Great Humbug   157

XVII   How the Balloon was Launched   165

XVIII   Away to the South   171

XIX   Attacked by the Fighting Trees   179

XX   The Dainty China Country   185

XXI   The Lion Becomes the King of Beasts   193

XXII   The Country of the Quadlings   199

XXIII   The Good Witch Grants Dorothy's Wish   205

XXIV   Home Again   213

This book is dedicated to my good friend & comrade. My Wife L.F.B.

# Chapter I.
# The Cyclone.

**D**orothy lived in the midst of the great Kansas prairies, with Uncle Henry, who was a farmer, and Aunt Em, who was the farmer's wife. Their house was small, for the lumber to build it had to be carried by wagon many miles. There were four walls, a floor and a roof, which made one room; and this room contained a rusty looking cooking stove, a cupboard for the dishes, a table, three or four chairs, and the beds. Uncle Henry and Aunt Em had a big bed in one corner, and Dorothy a little bed in another corner. There was no garret at all, and no cellar—except a small hole, dug in the ground, called a cyclone cellar, where the family could go in case one of those great whirlwinds arose, mighty enough to crush any building in its path. It was reached by a trap-door in the middle of the floor, from which a ladder led down into the small, dark hole.

When Dorothy stood in the doorway and looked around, she could see nothing but the great gray prairie on every side. Not a tree nor a house broke the broad sweep of flat country that reached the edge of the sky in all directions. The sun had baked the plowed land into a gray mass, with little cracks running through it. Even the grass was not green, for the sun had burned the tops of the long blades until they were the same gray color to be seen everywhere. Once the house had been painted, but the sun blistered the paint and the rains washed it away, and now the house was as dull and gray as everything else.[1]

When Aunt Em came there to live she was a young, pretty wife. The sun and wind had changed her, too. They had taken the sparkle from her eyes and left them a sober gray; they had taken the red from her cheeks and lips, and they were gray also. She was thin and gaunt, and never smiled, now. When Dorothy, who was an orphan, first came to her, Aunt Em had been so startled by the child's laughter that she would scream and press her hand upon her heart whenever Dorothy's merry voice reached her ears; and she still looked at the little girl with wonder that she could find anything to laugh at.

Uncle Henry never laughed. He worked hard from morning till night and did not know what joy was. He was gray also, from his long beard to his rough boots, and he looked stern and solemn, and rarely spoke.

It was Toto that made Dorothy laugh, and saved her from growing as gray as her other surroundings. Toto was not gray; he was a little black dog, with long, silky hair and small black eyes that twinkled merrily on either side of his funny, wee nose. Toto played all day long, and Dorothy played with him, and loved him dearly.

To-day, however, they were not playing. Uncle Henry sat upon the door-step and looked anxiously at the sky, which was even grayer than usual. Dorothy stood in the door with Toto in her arms, and looked at the sky too. Aunt Em was washing the dishes.

From the far north they heard a low wail of the wind, and Uncle Henry and Dorothy could see where the long grass bowed in waves before the coming storm. There now came a sharp whistling in the air from the south, and as they turned their eyes that way they saw ripples in the grass coming from that direction also.

Suddenly Uncle Henry stood up.

"There's a cyclone[2] coming, Em," he called to his wife; "I'll go look after the stock." Then he ran toward the sheds where the cows and horses were kept.

Aunt Em dropped her work and came to the door. One glance told her of the danger close at hand.

"Quick, Dorothy!" she screamed; "run for the cellar!"

Toto jumped out of Dorothy's arms and hid under the bed, and the girl started to get him. Aunt Em, badly frightened, threw open the trap-door in the floor and climbed down the ladder into the small, dark hole. Dorothy caught Toto at last, and started to follow her aunt. When she was half way across the room there came a great shriek from the wind, and the house shook so hard that she lost her footing and sat down suddenly upon the floor.

A strange thing then happened.

The house whirled around two or three times and rose slowly through the air. Dorothy felt as if she were going up in a balloon.

The north and south winds met where the house stood, and made it the exact center of the cyclone. In the middle of a cyclone the air is generally still, but the great pressure of the wind on every side of the house raised it up higher and higher, until it was at the very top of the cyclone; and there it remained and was carried miles and miles away as easily as you could carry a feather.

It was very dark, and the wind howled horribly around her, but Dorothy found she was riding quite easily. After the first few whirls around, and one other time when the house tipped badly, she felt as if she were being rocked gently, like a baby in a cradle.

Toto did not like it. He ran about the room, now here, now there, barking loudly; but Dorothy sat quite still on the floor and waited to see what would happen.

Once Toto got too near the open trap-door, and fell in; and at first the little girl thought she had lost him. But soon she saw one of his ears sticking up through the hole, for the strong pressure of the air was keeping him up so that he could not fall. She crept to the hole, caught Toto by the ear, and dragged him into the room again; afterward closing the trap-door so that no more accidents could happen.

Hour after hour passed away, and slowly Dorothy got over her fright; but she felt quite lonely, and the wind shrieked so loudly all about her that she nearly became deaf. At first she had wondered if she would be dashed to pieces when the house fell again; but as the hours passed and nothing terrible happened, she stopped worrying and resolved to wait calmly and see what the future would bring. At

*She caught Toto by the ear.*

last she crawled over the swaying floor to her bed, and lay down upon it; and Toto followed and lay down beside her.

In spite of the swaying of the house and the wailing of the wind, Dorothy soon closed her eyes and fell fast asleep.

# Chapter II.
# The Council with
# The Munchkins.

*Let Dorothy go to the City of Emeralds!*

**S**he was awakened by a shock, so sudden and severe that if Dorothy had not been lying on the soft bed she might have been hurt. As it was, the jar made her catch her breath and wonder what had happened; and Toto put his cold little nose into her face and whined dismally. Dorothy sat up and noticed that the house was not moving; nor was it dark, for the bright sunshine came in at the window, flooding the little room. She sprang from her bed and with Toto at her heels ran and opened the door.

The little girl gave a cry of amazement and looked about her, her eyes growing bigger and bigger at the wonderful sights she saw.

The cyclone had set the house down, very gently—for a cyclone—in the midst of a country of marvelous beauty. There were lovely patches of green sward all about, with stately trees bearing rich and luscious fruits. Banks of gorgeous flowers were on every hand, and birds with rare and brilliant plumage sang and fluttered in the trees and bushes. A little way off was a small brook, rushing and sparkling along between green banks, and murmuring in a voice very grateful to a little girl who had lived so long on the dry, gray prairies.[3]

While she stood looking eagerly at the strange and beautiful sights, she noticed coming toward her a group of the queerest people she had ever seen. They were not as big as the grown folk she had always been used to; but neither were they very small. In fact, they seemed about as tall as Dorothy, who was a well-grown child for her age, although they were, so far as looks go, many years older.

Three were men and one a woman, and all were oddly dressed. They wore round hats that rose to a small point a foot above their heads, with little bells around the brims that tinkled sweetly as they moved. The hats of the men were blue; the little woman's hat was white,[4] and she wore a white gown that hung in plaits from her shoulders; over it were sprinkled little stars that glistened in the sun like diamonds. The men were dressed in blue, of the same shade as their hats, and wore well polished boots with a deep roll of blue at the tops. The men, Dorothy thought, were about as old as Uncle Henry, for two of them had beards. But the little woman was doubtless much older: her face was covered with wrinkles, her hair was nearly white, and she walked rather stiffly.

When these people drew near the house where Dorothy was standing in the doorway, they paused and whispered among themselves, as if afraid to come farther. But the little old woman walked up to Dorothy, made a low bow and said, in a sweet voice,

"You are welcome, most noble Sorceress, to the land of the Munchkins. We are so grateful to you for having killed the wicked Witch of the East, and for setting our people free from bondage."

Dorothy listened to this speech with wonder. What could the little woman possibly mean by calling her a sorceress, and saying she had killed the wicked Witch of the East? Dorothy was an innocent, harmless little girl, who had been carried by a cyclone many miles from home; and she had never killed anything in all her life.

But the little woman evidently expected her to answer; so Dorothy said, with hesitation,

"You are very kind; but there must be some mistake. I have not killed anything."

"Your house did, anyway," replied the little old woman, with a laugh; "and that is the same thing. See!" she continued, pointing to the corner of the house; "there are her two toes still sticking out from under a block of wood."

Dorothy looked and gave a little cry of fright. There, indeed, just under the corner of the great beam the house rested on, two feet were sticking out, shod in silver shoes with pointed toes.

"Oh, dear! oh, dear!" cried Dorothy, clasping her hands together in dismay; "the house must have fallen on her. What ever shall we do?"

"There is nothing to be done," said the little woman, calmly.

"But who was she?" asked Dorothy.

"She was the wicked Witch of the East, as I said," answered the little woman. "She has held all the Munchkins in bondage for many years, making them slave for her night and day. Now they are all set free, and are grateful to you for the favour."

"Who are the Munchkins?" enquired Dorothy.

"They are the people who live in this land of the East, where the wicked Witch ruled."

"Are you a Munchkin?" asked Dorothy.

"No; but I am their friend, although I live in the land of the North. When they saw the Witch of the East was dead the Munchkins sent a swift messenger to me, and I came at once. I am the Witch of the North."

"Oh, gracious!" cried Dorothy; "are you a real witch?"

"Yes, indeed;" answered the little woman. "But I am a good witch, and the people love me. I am not as powerful as the wicked Witch was who ruled here, or I should have set the people free myself."

"But I thought all witches were wicked,"[5] said the girl, who was half frightened at facing a real witch.

"Oh, no; that is a great mistake. There were only four witches in all the Land of Oz, and two of them, those who live in the North and the South, are good witches. I know this is true, for I am one of them myself, and cannot be mistaken. Those who dwelt in the East and the West were, indeed, wicked witches; but now that you have killed one of them, there is but one wicked Witch in all the Land of Oz—the one who lives in the West."

*"I am the Witch of the North."*

"But," said Dorothy, after a moment's thought, "Aunt Em has told me that the witches were all dead—years and years ago."

"Who is Aunt Em?" inquired the little old woman.

"She is my aunt who lives in Kansas, where I came from."

The Witch of the North seemed to think for a time, with her head bowed and her eyes upon the ground. Then she looked up and said,

"I do not know where Kansas is, for I have never heard that country mentioned before. But tell me, is it a civilized country?"

"Oh, yes;" replied Dorothy.

"Then that accounts for it. In the civilized countries I believe there are no witches left; nor wizards, nor sorceresses, nor magicians. But, you see, the Land of Oz has never been civilized, for we are cut off from all the rest of the world. Therefore we still have witches and wizards amongst us."

"Who are the Wizards?" asked Dorothy.

"Oz himself is the Great Wizard," answered the Witch, sinking her voice to a whisper. "He is more powerful than all the rest of us together. He lives in the City of Emeralds."

Dorothy was going to ask another question, but just then the Munchkins, who had been standing silently by, gave a loud shout and pointed to the corner of the house where the Wicked Witch had been lying.

"What is it?" asked the little old woman; and looked, and began to laugh. The feet of the dead Witch had disappeared entirely and nothing was left but the silver shoes.

"She was so old," explained the Witch of the North, "that she dried up quickly in the sun. That is the end of her. But the silver shoes are yours, and you shall have them to wear." She reached down and picked up the shoes, and after shaking the dust out of them handed them to Dorothy.

"The Witch of the East was proud of those silver shoes," said one of the Munchkins; "and there is some charm connected with them; but what it is we never knew."

Dorothy carried the shoes into the house and placed them on the table. Then she came out again to the Munchkins and said,

"I am anxious to get back to my Aunt and Uncle, for I am sure they will worry about me. Can you help me find my way?"

The Munchkins and the Witch first looked at one another, and then at Dorothy, and then shook their heads.

"At the East, not far from here," said one, "there is a great desert, and none could live to cross it."

"It is the same at the South," said another, "for I have been there and seen it. The South is the country of the Quadlings."

"I am told," said the third man, "that it is the same at the West. And that country, where the Winkies live, is ruled by the wicked Witch of the West, who would make you her slave if you passed her way."

"The North is my home," said the old lady, "and at its edge is the same great desert that surrounds this land of Oz. I'm afraid, my dear, you will have to live with us."

Dorothy began to sob, at this, for she felt lonely among all these strange people. Her tears seemed to grieve the kind-hearted Munchkins, for they immediately took out their handkerchiefs and began to weep also. As for the little old woman, she took off her cap and balanced the point on the end of her nose, while she counted "one, two, three" in a solemn voice. At once the cap changed to a slate, on which was written in big, white chalk marks:

"LET DOROTHY GO TO THE CITY OF EMERALDS."

The little old woman took the slate from her nose, and, having read the words on it, asked,

"Is your name Dorothy, my dear?"

"Yes," answered the child, looking up and drying her tears.

"Then you must go to the City of Emeralds. Perhaps Oz will help you."

"Where is this City?" asked Dorothy.

"It is exactly in the center of the country, and is ruled by Oz, the Great Wizard I told you of."

"Is he a good man?" enquired the girl, anxiously.

"He is a good Wizard. Whether he is a man or not I cannot tell, for I have never seen him."

"How can I get there?" asked Dorothy

"You must walk. It is a long journey, through a country that is sometimes pleasant and sometimes dark and terrible. However, I will use all the magic arts I know of to keep you from harm."

"Won't you go with me?" pleaded the girl, who had begun to look upon the little old woman as her only friend.

"No, I cannot do that," she replied; "but I will give you my kiss, and no one will dare injure a person who has been kissed by the Witch of the North."

She came close to Dorothy and kissed her gently on the forehead. Where her lips touched the girl they left a round, shining mark, as Dorothy found out soon after.

"The road to the City of Emeralds is paved with yellow brick,"[6] said the Witch; "so you cannot miss it. When you get to Oz do not be afraid of him, but tell your story and ask him to help you. Good-bye, my dear."

The three Munchkins bowed low to her and wished her a pleasant journey, after which they walked away through the trees. The Witch gave Dorothy a friendly little nod, whirled around on her left heel three times, and straightway disappeared, much to the surprise of little Toto, who barked after her loudly enough when she had gone, because he had been afraid even to growl while she stood by.

But Dorothy, knowing her to be a witch, had expected her to disappear in just that way, and was not surprised in the least.

# Chapter III
## How Dorothy saved
## the Scarecrow.

**W**hen Dorothy was left alone she began to feel hungry. So she went to the cupboard and cut herself some bread, which she spread with butter. She gave some to Toto, and taking a pail from the shelf she carried it down to the little brook and filled it with clear, sparkling water. Toto ran over to the trees and began to bark at the birds sitting there. Dorothy went to get him, and saw such delicious fruit hanging from the branches that she gathered some of it, finding it just what she wanted to help out her breakfast.

Then she went back to the house, and having helped herself and Toto to a good drink of the cool, clear water, she set about making ready for the journey to the City of Emeralds.

Dorothy had only one other dress, but that happened to be clean and was hanging on a peg beside her bed. It was gingham, with checks of white and blue[7] and although the blue was somewhat faded with many washings, it was still a pretty frock. The girl washed herself carefully, dressed herself in the clean gingham, and tied her pink sunbonnet on her head. She took a little basket and filled it with bread from the cupboard, laying a white cloth over the top. Then she looked down at her feet and noticed how old and worn her shoes were.

"They surely will never do for a long journey, Toto," she said. And Toto looked up into her face with his little black eyes and wagged his tail to show he knew what she meant.

At that moment Dorothy saw lying on the table the silver shoes that had belonged to the Witch of the East.

"I wonder if they will fit me," she said to Toto. "They would be just the thing to take a long walk in, for they could not wear out."

She took off her old leather shoes and tried on the silver ones, which fitted her as well as if they had been made for her.[8]

Finally she picked up her basket.

"Come along, Toto," she said, "we will go to the Emerald City and ask the great Oz how to get back to Kansas again."

She closed the door, locked it, and put the key carefully in the pocket of her dress. And so, with Toto trotting along soberly behind her, she started on her journey.

There were several roads near by, but it did not take her long to find the one paved with yellow brick.[9] Within a short time she was walking briskly toward the Emerald City, her silver shoes tinkling merrily on the hard, yellow roadbed. The sun shone bright and the birds sang sweet and Dorothy did not feel nearly as bad as you might think a little girl would who had been suddenly whisked away from her own country and set down in the midst of a strange land.

She was surprised, as she walked along, to see how pretty the country was about her. There were neat fences at the sides of the road, painted a dainty blue color, and beyond them were fields of grain and vegetables in abundance. Evidently the Munchkins were good farmers and able to raise large crops. Once in a while she would pass a house, and the people came out to look at her and bow low as she went by; for everyone knew she had been the means of destroying the wicked witch and setting them free from bondage. The Houses of the Munchkins were odd looking dwellings, for each was round, with a big dome for a roof. All were painted blue, for in this country of the East blue was the favorite color.

Towards evening, when Dorothy was tired with her long walk and began to wonder where she should pass the night, she came to a house rather larger than the rest. On the green lawn before it many men and women were dancing. Five little fiddlers played as loudly as possible and the people were laughing and singing, while a big table near by was loaded with delicious fruits and nuts, pies and cakes, and many other good things to eat.

The people greeted Dorothy kindly, and invited her to supper and to pass the night with them; for this was the home of one of the richest Munchkins in the land, and his friends were gathered with him to celebrate their freedom from the bondage of the wicked witch.

Dorothy ate a hearty supper and was waited upon by the rich Munchkin himself, whose name was Boq. Then she sat down upon a settee and watched the people dance.

When Boq saw her silver shoes he said,

"You must be a great sorceress."

"Why?" asked the girl.

"Because you wear silver shoes and have killed the wicked witch. Besides, you have white in your frock, and only witches and sorceresses wear white."

"My dress is blue and white checked," said Dorothy, smoothing out the wrinkles in it.

"It is kind of you to wear that," said Boq. "Blue is the color of the Munchkins, and white is the witch color; so we know you are a friendly witch."

Dorothy did not know what to say to this, for all the people seemed to think her a witch, and she knew very well she was only an ordinary little girl who had come by the chance of a cyclone into a strange land.

When she had tired watching the dancing, Boq led her into the house, where he gave her a room with a pretty bed in it. The sheets were made of blue cloth, and Dorothy slept soundly in them till morning, with Toto curled up on the blue rug beside her.

She ate a hearty breakfast, and watched a wee Munchkin baby, who played with Toto and pulled his tail and crowed and laughed in a way that greatly amused Dorothy. Toto was a fine curiosity to all the people, for they had never seen a dog before.

"How far is it to the Emerald City?" the girl asked.

"I do not know," answered Boq, gravely, "for I have never been

*"You must be a great sorceress."*

there. It is better for people to keep away from Oz, unless they have business with him. But it is a long way to the Emerald City, and it will take you many days. The country here is rich and pleasant, but you must pass through rough and dangerous places before you reach the end of your journey."

This worried Dorothy a little, but she knew that only the great Oz could help her get to Kansas again, so she bravely resolved not to turn back.

She bade her friends good-bye, and again started along the road of yellow brick. When she had gone several miles she thought she would stop to rest, and so climbed to the top of the fence beside the road and sat down. There was a great cornfield beyond the fence, and not far away she saw a Scarecrow, placed high on a pole to keep the birds from the ripe corn.

Dorothy leaned her chin upon her hand and gazed thoughtfully at the Scarecrow. Its head was a small sack stuffed with straw, with eyes, nose and mouth painted on it to represent a face. An old, pointed blue hat, that had belonged to some Munchkin, was perched on this head, and the rest of the figure was a blue suit of clothes, worn and faded, which had also been stuffed with straw. On the feet were some old boots with blue tops, such as every man wore in this country, and the figure was raised above the stalks of corn by means of the pole stuck up its back.

While Dorothy was looking earnestly into the queer, painted face of the Scarecrow, she was surprised to see one of the eyes slowly wink at her. She thought she must have been mistaken, at first, for none of the scarecrows in Kansas ever wink; but presently the figure nodded its head to her in a friendly way. Then she climbed down from the fence and walked up to it, while Toto ran around the pole and barked.

"Good day," said the Scarecrow, in a rather husky voice.

"Did you speak?" asked the girl, in wonder.

"Certainly," answered the Scarecrow; "how do you do?"

"I'm pretty well, thank you," replied Dorothy, politely; "how do you do?"

"I'm not feeling well," said the Scarecrow, with a smile, "for it is very tedious being perched up here night and day to scare away crows."

*Dorothy gazed thoughtfully at the Scarecrow.*

"Can't you get down?" asked Dorothy.

"No, for this pole is stuck up my back. If you will please take away the pole I shall be greatly obliged to you."

Dorothy reached up both arms and lifted the figure off the pole; for, being stuffed with straw, it was quite light.

"Thank you very much," said the Scarecrow, when he had been set down on the ground. "I feel like a new man."

Dorothy was puzzled at this, for it sounded queer to hear a stuffed man speak, and to see him bow and walk along beside her.

"Who are you?" asked the Scarecrow, when he had stretched himself and yawned, "and where are you going?"

"My name is Dorothy," said the girl, "and I am going to the Emerald City, to ask the great Oz to send me back to Kansas."

"Where is the Emerald City?" he enquired; "and who is Oz?"

"Why, don't you know?" she returned, in surprise.

"No, indeed; I don't know anything. You see, I am stuffed, so I have no brains at all," he answered, sadly.

"Oh," said Dorothy; "I'm awfully sorry for you."

"Do you think," he asked, "if I go to the Emerald City with you, that the great Oz would give me some brains?"

"I cannot tell," she returned; "but you may come with me, if you like. If Oz will not give you any brains you will be no worse off than you are now."

"That is true," said the Scarecrow. "You see," he continued, confidentially, "I don't mind my legs and arms and body being stuffed, because I cannot get hurt. If anyone treads on my toes or sticks a pin into me, it doesn't matter, for I can't feel it. But I do not want people to call me a fool, and if my head stays stuffed with straw instead of with brains, as yours is, how am I ever to know anything?"

"I understand how you feel," said the little girl, who was truly sorry for him. "If you will come with me I'll ask Oz to do all he can for you."

"Thank you," he answered, gratefully.

They walked back to the road, Dorothy helped him over the fence, and they started along the path of yellow brick for the Emerald City.

Toto did not like this addition to the party, at first. He smelled around the stuffed man as if he suspected there might be a nest of rats in the straw, and he often growled in an unfriendly way at the Scarecrow.

"Don't mind Toto," said Dorothy, to her new friend; "he never bites."

"Oh, I'm not afraid," replied the Scarecrow, "he can't hurt the straw. Do let me carry that basket for you. I shall not mind it, for I can't get tired. I'll tell you a secret," he continued, as he walked along; "there is only one thing in the world I am afraid of."

"What is that?" asked Dorothy; "the Munchkin farmer who made you?"

"No," answered the Scarecrow; "it's a lighted match."

# Chapter IV.
## ~The Road through the Forest~

# After

a few hours the road began to be rough, and the walking grew so difficult that the Scarecrow often stumbled over the yellow brick, which were here very uneven. Sometimes, indeed, they were broken or missing altogether, leaving holes that Toto jumped across and Dorothy walked around. As for the Scarecrow, having no brains he walked straight ahead, and so stepped into the holes and fell at full length on the hard bricks. It never hurt him, however, and Dorothy would pick him up and set him upon his feet again, while he joined her in laughing merrily at his own mishap.

The farms were not nearly so well cared for here as they were farther back. There were fewer houses and fewer fruit trees, and the farther they went the more dismal and lonesome the country became.

At noon they sat down by the roadside, near a little brook, and Dorothy opened her basket and got out some bread. She offered a piece to the Scarecrow, but he refused.

"I am never hungry," he said; "and it is a lucky thing I am not. For my mouth is only painted, and if I should cut a hole in it so

I could eat, the straw I am stuffed with would come out, and that would spoil the shape of my head."

Dorothy saw at once that this was true, so she only nodded and went on eating her bread.

"Tell me something about yourself, and the country you came from," said the Scarecrow, when she had finished her dinner. So she told him all about Kansas, and how gray everything was there, and how the cyclone had carried her to this queer land of Oz. The Scarecrow listened carefully, and said,

"I cannot understand why you should wish to leave this beautiful country and go back to the dry, gray place you call Kansas."

"That is because you have no brains," answered the girl. "No matter how dreary and gray our homes are, we people of flesh and blood would rather live there than in any other country, be it ever so beautiful. There is no place like home."

The Scarecrow sighed.

"Of course I cannot understand it," he said. "If your heads were stuffed with straw, like mine, you would probably all live in the beautiful places, and then Kansas would have no people at all. It is fortunate for Kansas that you have brains."

"Won't you tell me a story, while we are resting?" asked the child.

The Scarecrow looked at her reproachfully, and answered,

"My life has been so short that I really know nothing whatever. I was only made day before yesterday. What happened in the world before that time is all unknown to me. Luckily, when the farmer made my head, one of the first things he did was to paint my ears, so that I heard what was going on. There was another Munchkin with him, and the first thing I heard was the farmer saying,

" 'How do you like those ears?'

" 'They aren't straight,' answered the other.

" 'Never mind,' said the farmer; 'they are ears just the same,' which was true enough.

" 'Now I'll make the eyes,' said the farmer. So he painted my right eye, and as soon as it was finished I found myself looking at him and at everything around me with a great deal of curiosity, for this was my first glimpse of the world.

" 'That's a rather pretty eye,' remarked the Munchkin who was watching the farmer; 'blue paint is just the color for eyes.'

*"I was only made yesterday,"* said the Scarecrow.

" 'I think I'll make the other a little bigger,' said the farmer; and when the second eye was done I could see much better than before. Then he made my nose and my mouth; but I did not speak, because at that time I didn't know what a mouth was for. I had the fun of watching them make my body and my arms and legs; and when they fastened on my head, at last, I felt very proud, for I thought I was just as good a man as anyone.

" 'This fellow will scare the crows fast enough,' said the farmer; 'he looks just like a man.'

" 'Why, he is a man,' said the other, and I quite agreed with him. The farmer carried me under his arm to the cornfield, and set me up on a tall stick, where you found me. He and his friend soon after walked away and left me alone.

"I did not like to be deserted this way; so I tried to walk after them, but my feet would not touch the ground, and I was forced to stay on that pole. It was a lonely life to lead, for I had nothing to think of, having been made such a little while before. Many crows and other birds flew into the cornfield, but as soon as they saw me they flew away again, thinking I was a Munchkin; and this pleased me and made me feel that I was quite an important person. By and by an old crow flew near me, and after looking at me carefully he perched upon my shoulder and said,

" 'I wonder if that farmer thought to fool me in this clumsy manner. Any crow of sense could see that you are only stuffed with straw.' Then he hopped down at my feet and ate all the corn he wanted. The other birds, seeing he was not harmed by me, came to eat the corn too, so in a short time there was a great flock of them about me.

"I felt sad at this, for it showed I was not such a good Scarecrow after all; but the old crow comforted me, saying: 'If you only had brains in your head you would be as good a man as any of them, and a better man than some of them. Brains are the only things worth having in this world, no matter whether one is a crow or a man.'

"After the crows had gone I thought this over, and decided I would try hard to get some brains. By good luck, you came along and pulled me off the stake, and from what you say I am sure the great Oz will give me brains as soon as we get to the Emerald City."

"I hope so," said Dorothy, earnestly, "since you seem anxious to have them."

"Oh yes; I am anxious," returned the Scarecrow. "It is such an uncomfortable feeling to know one is a fool."

"Well," said the girl, "let us go." And she handed the basket to the Scarecrow.

There were no fences at all by the road side now, and the land was rough and untilled. Towards evening they came to a great forest, where the trees grew so big and close together that their branches met over the road of yellow brick. It was almost dark under the trees, for the branches shut out the daylight; but the travellers did not stop, and went on into the forest.

"If this road goes in, it must come out," said the Scarecrow, "and as the Emerald City is at the other end of the road, we must go wherever it leads us."

"Anyone would know that," said Dorothy.

"Certainly; that is why I know it," returned the Scarecrow. "If it required brains to figure it out, I never should have said it."

After an hour or so the light faded away, and they found themselves stumbling along in the darkness. Dorothy could not see at all, but Toto could, for some dogs see very well in the dark; and the Scarecrow declared he could see as well as by day. So she took hold of his arm, and managed to get along fairly well.

"If you see any house, or any place where we can pass the night," she said, "you must tell me; for it is very uncomfortable walking in the dark."

Soon after the Scarecrow stopped.

"I see a little cottage at the right of us," he said, "built of logs and branches. Shall we go there?"

"Yes, indeed;" answered the child. "I am all tired out."

So the Scarecrow led her through the trees until they reached the cottage, and Dorothy entered and found a bed of dried leaves in one corner. She lay down at once, and with Toto beside her soon fell into a sound sleep. The Scarecrow, who was never tired, stood up in another corner and waited patiently until morning came.

# Chapter V.
# The Rescue of
# the Tin Woodman

**W**hen Dorothy awoke the sun was shining through the trees and Toto had long been out chasing birds and squirrels. She sat up and looked around her. There was the Scarecrow, still standing patiently in his corner, waiting for her.

"We must go and search for water," she said to him.

"Why do you want water?" he asked.

"To wash my face clean after the dust of the road, and to drink, so the dry bread will not stick in my throat."

"It must be inconvenient to be made of flesh," said the Scarecrow, thoughtfully; "for you must sleep, and eat and drink. However, you have brains, and it is worth a lot of bother to be able to think properly."

They left the cottage and walked through the trees until they found a little spring of clear water, where Dorothy drank and bathed and ate her breakfast. She saw there was not much bread left in the basket, and the girl was thankful the Scarecrow did not have to eat anything, for there was scarcely enough for herself and Toto for the day.

When she had finished her meal, and was about to go back to the road of yellow brick, she was startled to hear a deep groan near by.

"What was that?" she asked, timidly.

"I cannot imagine," replied the Scarecrow; "but we can go and see."

Just then another groan reached their ears, and the sound seemed to come from behind them. They turned and walked through the forest a few steps, when Dorothy discovered something shining in a ray of sunshine that fell between the trees. She ran to the place, and then stopped short, with a cry of surprise.

One of the big trees had been partly chopped through, and standing beside it, with an uplifted axe in his hands, was a man made entirely of tin.[10] His head and arms and legs were jointed upon his body, but he stood perfectly motionless, as if he could not stir at all.

Dorothy looked at him in amazement, and so did the Scarecrow, while Toto barked sharply and made a snap at the tin legs, which hurt his teeth.

"Did you groan?" asked Dorothy.

"Yes," answered the tin man; "I did. I've been groaning for more than a year, and no one has ever heard me before or come to help me."

"What can I do for you?" she enquired, softly, for she was moved by the sad voice in which the man spoke.

"Get an oil-can and oil my joints," he answered. "They are rusted so badly that I cannot move them at all; if I am well oiled I shall soon be all right again. You will find an oil-can on a shelf in my cottage."

Dorothy at once ran back to the cottage and found the oil-can, and then she returned and asked, anxiously, "Where are your joints?"

"Oil my neck, first," replied the Tin Woodman. So she oiled it, and as it was quite badly rusted the Scarecrow took hold of the tin head and moved it gently from side to side until it worked freely, and then the man could turn it himself.

"Now oil the joints in my arms," he said. And Dorothy oiled

them and the Scarecrow bent them carefully until they were quite free from rust and as good as new.

The Tin Woodman gave a sigh of satisfaction and lowered his axe, which he leaned against the tree.

"This is a great comfort," he said. "I have been holding that axe in the air ever since I rusted, and I'm glad to be able to put it down at last. Now, if you will oil the joints of my legs, I shall be all right once more."

So they oiled his legs until he could move them freely; and he thanked them again and again for his release, for he seemed a very polite creature, and very grateful.

"I might have stood there always if you had not come along," he said; "so you have certainly saved my life. How did you happen to be here?"

"We are on our way to the Emerald City, to see the great Oz," she answered, "and we stopped at your cottage to pass the night."

"Why do you wish to see Oz?" he asked.

"I want him to send me back to Kansas; and the Scarecrow wants him to put a few brains into his head," she replied.

The Tin Woodman appeared to think deeply for a moment. Then he said:

"Do you suppose Oz could give me a heart?"

"Why, I guess so," Dorothy answered; "it would be as easy as to give the Scarecrow brains."

"True," the Tin Woodman returned. "So, if you will allow me to join your party, I will also go to the Emerald City and ask Oz to help me."

"Come along," said the Scarecrow, heartily; and Dorothy added that she would be pleased to have his company. So the Tin Woodman shouldered his axe and they all passed through the forest until they came to the road that was paved with yellow brick.

The Tin Woodman had asked Dorothy to put the oil-can in her basket. "For," he said, "if I should get caught in the rain, and rust again, I would need the oil-can badly."

It was a bit of good luck to have their new comrade join the party, for soon after they had begun their journey again they came to a place where the trees and branches grew so thick over the road that the travellers could not pass. But the Tin Woodman set to work

*"This is a great comfort," said the Tin Woodman.*

with his axe and chopped so well that soon he cleared a passage for the entire party.

Dorothy was thinking so earnestly as they walked along that she did not notice when the Scarecrow stumbled into a hole and rolled over to the side of the road. Indeed, he was obliged to call to her to help him up again.

"Why didn't you walk around the hole?" asked the Tin Woodman.

"I don't know enough," replied the Scarecrow, cheerfully. "My head is stuffed with straw, you know, and that is why I am going to Oz to ask him for some brains."

"Oh, I see;" said the Tin Woodman. "But, after all, brains are not the best things in the world."

"Have you any?" enquired the Scarecrow.

"No, my head is quite empty," answered the Woodman; "but once I had brains, and a heart also; so, having tried them both, I should much rather have a heart."

"And why is that?" asked the Scarecrow.

"I will tell you my story, and then you will know."

So, while they were walking through the forest, the Tin Woodman told the following story:

"I was born the son of a woodman who chopped down trees in the forest and sold the wood for a living. When I grew up I too became a wood-chopper, and after my father died I took care of my old mother as long as she lived. Then I made up my mind that instead of living alone I would marry, so that I might not become lonely.

"There was one of the Munchkin girls who was so beautiful that I soon grew to love her with all my heart. She, on her part, promised to marry me as soon as I could earn enough money to build a better house for her; so I set to work harder than ever. But the girl lived with an old woman[11] who did not want her to marry anyone, for she was so lazy she wished the girl to remain with her and do the cooking and the housework. So the old woman went to the wicked Witch of the East, and promised her two sheep and a cow if she would prevent the marriage. Thereupon the wicked Witch enchanted my axe, and when I was chopping away at my best one day, for I was anxious to get the new house and my wife as soon as possible, the axe slipped all at once and cut off my left leg.

"This at first seemed a great misfortune, for I knew a one-legged man could not do very well as a wood-chopper. So I went to a tin-smith and had him make me a new leg out of tin. The leg worked very well, once I was used to it; but my action angered the wicked Witch of the East, for she had promised the old woman I should not marry the pretty Munchkin girl. When I began chopping again my axe slipped and cut off my right leg. Again I went to the tinner, and again he made me a leg out of tin. After this the enchanted axe cut off my arms, one after the other; but, nothing daunted, I had them replaced with tin ones. The wicked Witch then made the axe slip and cut off my head, and at first I thought that was the end of me. But the tinner happened to come along, and he made me a new head out of tin.

"I thought I had beaten the wicked Witch then, and I worked harder than ever; but I little knew how cruel my enemy could be. She thought of a new way to kill my love for the beautiful Munchkin maiden, and made my axe slip again, so that it cut right through my body, splitting me into two halves. Once more the tinner came to my help and made me a body of tin, fastening my tin arms and legs and head to it, by means of joints, so that I could move around as well as ever. But, alas! I had now no heart, so that I lost all my love for the Munchkin girl, and did not care whether I married her or not. I suppose she is still living with the old woman, waiting for me to come after her.

"My body shone so brightly in the sun that I felt very proud of it and it did not matter now if my axe slipped, for it could not cut me. There was only one danger—that my joints would rust; but I kept an oil-can in my cottage and took care to oil myself whenever I needed it. However, there came a day when I forgot to do this, and, being caught in a rainstorm, before I thought of the danger my joints had rusted, and I was left to stand in the woods until you came to help me. It was a terrible thing to undergo, but during the year I stood there I had time to think that the greatest loss I had known was the loss of my heart. While I was in love I was the happiest man on earth; but no one can love who has not a heart, and so I am resolved to ask Oz to give me one. If he does, I will go back to the Munchkin maiden and marry her."

Both Dorothy and the Scarecrow had been greatly interested in the story of the Tin Woodman, and now they knew why he was so anxious to get a new heart.

"All the same," said the Scarecrow, "I shall ask for brains instead of a heart; for a fool would not know what to do with a heart if he had one."

"I shall take the heart," returned the Tin Woodman; "for brains do not make one happy, and happiness is the best thing in the world."

Dorothy did not say anything, for she was puzzled to know which of her two friends was right, and she decided if she could only get back to Kansas and Aunt Em it did not matter so much whether the Woodman had no brains and the Scarecrow no heart, or each got what he wanted.

What worried her most was that the bread was nearly gone, and another meal for herself and Toto would empty the basket. To be sure neither the Woodman nor the Scarecrow ever ate anything, but she was not made of tin nor straw, and could not live unless she was fed.

**A**ll this time Dorothy and her companions had been walking through the thick woods. The road was still paved with yellow brick, but these were much covered by dried branches and dead leaves from the trees, and the walking was not at all good.

There were few birds in this part of the forest, for birds love the open country where there is plenty of sunshine; but now and then there came a deep growl from some wild animal hidden among the trees. These sounds made the little girl's heart beat fast, for she did not know what made them; but Toto knew, and he walked close to Dorothy's side, and did not even bark in return.

"How long will it be," the child asked of the Tin Woodman, "before we are out of the forest?"

"I cannot tell," was the answer, "for I have never been to the Emerald City. But my father went there once, when I was a boy, and he said it was a long journey through a dangerous country, although nearer to the city where Oz dwells the country is beautiful. But I am not afraid so long as I have my oil-can, and nothing can hurt the Scarecrow, while you bear upon your forehead the mark of the good Witch's kiss, and that will protect you from harm."

"But Toto!" said the girl, anxiously; "what will protect him?"

"We must protect him ourselves, if he is in danger," replied the Tin Woodman.

Just as he spoke there came from the forest a terrible roar, and the next moment a great Lion bounded into the road. With one blow of his paw he sent the Scarecrow spinning over and over to the edge of the road, and then he struck at the Tin Woodman with his sharp claws. But, to the Lion's surprise, he could make no impression on the tin, although the Woodman fell over in the road and lay still.

Little Toto, now that he had an enemy to face, ran barking toward the Lion, and the great beast had opened his mouth to bite the dog, when Dorothy, fearing Toto would be killed, and heedless of danger, rushed forward and slapped the Lion upon his nose as hard as she could, while she cried out:

"Don't you dare to bite Toto! You ought to be ashamed of yourself, a big beast like you, to bite a poor little dog!"

"I didn't bite him," said the Lion, as he rubbed his nose with his paw where Dorothy had hit it.

"No, but you tried to," she retorted. "You are nothing but a big coward."

"I know it," said the Lion, hanging his head in shame; "I've always known it. But how can I help it?"

"I don't know, I'm sure. To think of your striking a stuffed man, like the poor Scarecrow!"

"Is he stuffed?" asked the Lion, in surprise, as he watched her pick up the Scarecrow and set him upon his feet, while she patted him into shape again.

"Of course he's stuffed," replied Dorothy, who was still angry.

"That's why he went over so easily," remarked the Lion. "It astonished me to see him whirl around so. Is the other one stuffed, also?"

"No," said Dorothy, "he's made of tin." And she helped the Woodman up again.

"That's why he nearly blunted my claws," said the Lion. "When they scratched against the tin it made a cold shiver run down my back. What is that little animal you are so tender of?"

"He is my dog, Toto," answered Dorothy.

"Is he made of tin, or stuffed?" asked the Lion.

*"You ought to be ashamed of yourself!"*

"Neither. He's a—a—a meat dog," said the girl.

"Oh. He's a curious animal, and seems remarkably small, now that I look at him. No one would think of biting such a little thing except a coward like me," continued the Lion, sadly.

"What makes you a coward?" asked Dorothy, looking at the great beast in wonder, for he was as big as a small horse.

"It's a mystery," replied the Lion. "I suppose I was born that way. All the other animals in the forest naturally expect me to be brave, for the Lion is everywhere thought to be the King of Beasts. I learned that if I roared very loudly every living thing was frightened and got out of my way. Whenever I've met a man I've been awfully scared; but I just roared at him, and he has always run away as fast as he could go. If the elephants and the tigers and the bears had ever tried to fight me, I should have run myself—I'm such a coward; but just as soon as they hear me roar they all try to get away from me, and of course I let them go."

"But that isn't right. The King of Beasts shouldn't be a coward," said the Scarecrow.

"I know it," returned the Lion, wiping a tear from his eye with the tip of his tail; "it is my great sorrow, and makes my life very unhappy. But whenever there is danger my heart begins to beat fast."

"Perhaps you have heart disease," said the Tin Woodman.

"It may be," said the Lion.

"If you have," continued the Tin Woodman, "you ought to be glad, for it proves you have a heart. For my part, I have no heart; so I cannot have heart disease."

"Perhaps," said the Lion, thoughtfully, "if I had no heart I should not be a coward."

"Have you brains?" asked the Scarecrow.

"I suppose so. I've never looked to see," replied the Lion.

"I am going to the great Oz to ask him to give me some," remarked the Scarecrow, "for my head is stuffed with straw."

"And I am going to ask him to give me a heart," said the Woodman.

"And I am going to ask him to send Toto and me back to Kansas," added Dorothy.

"Do you think Oz could give me courage?" asked the Cowardly Lion.

"Just as easily as he could give me brains," said the Scarecrow.

"Or give me a heart," said the Tin Woodman.

"Or send me back to Kansas," said Dorothy.

"Then, if you don't mind, I'll go with you," said the Lion, "for my life is simply unbearable without a bit of courage."

"You will be very welcome," answered Dorothy, "for you will help to keep away the other wild beasts. It seems to me they must be more cowardly than you[12] are if they allow you to scare them so easily."

"They really are," said the Lion; "but that doesn't make me any braver, and as long as I know myself to be a coward I shall be unhappy."

So once more the little company set off upon the journey, the Lion walking with stately strides at Dorothy's side. Toto did not approve this new comrade at first, for he could not forget how nearly he had been crushed between the Lion's great jaws; but after a time he became more at ease, and presently Toto and the Cowardly Lion had grown to be good friends.

During the rest of that day there was no other adventure to mar the peace of their journey. Once, indeed, the Tin Woodman stepped upon a beetle that was crawling along the road, and killed the poor little thing. This made the Tin Woodman very unhappy, for he was always careful not to hurt any living creature; and as he walked along he wept several tears of sorrow and regret. These tears ran slowly down his face and over the hinges of his jaw, and there they rusted. When Dorothy presently asked him a question the Tin Woodman could not open his mouth, for his jaws were tightly rusted together. He became greatly frightened at this and made many motions to Dorothy to relieve him, but she could not understand. The Lion was also puzzled to know what was wrong. But the Scarecrow seized the oil-can from Dorothy's basket and oiled the Woodman's jaws, so that after a few moments he could talk as well as before.

"This will serve me a lesson," said he, "to look where I step. For if I should kill another bug or beetle I should surely cry again, and crying rusts my jaw so that I cannot speak."

Thereafter he walked very carefully, with his eyes on the road, and when he saw a tiny ant toiling by he would step over it, so as not to harm it. The Tin Woodman knew very well he had no heart, and therefore he took great care never to be cruel or unkind to anything.

"You people with hearts," he said, "have something to guide you, and need never do wrong; but I have no heart, and so I must be very careful. When Oz gives me a heart of course I needn't mind so much."

**T**hey were obliged to camp out that night under a large tree in the forest, for there were no houses near. The tree made a good, thick covering to protect them from the dew, and the Tin Woodman chopped a great pile of wood with his axe and Dorothy built a splendid fire that warmed her and made her feel less lonely. She and Toto ate the last of their bread, and now she did not know what they would do for breakfast.

"If you wish," said the Lion, "I will go into the forest and kill a deer for you. You can roast it by the fire, since your tastes are so peculiar that you prefer cooked food, and then you will have a very good breakfast."

"Don't! please don't," begged the Tin Woodman. "I should certainly weep if you killed a poor deer, and then my jaws would rust again."

But the Lion went away into the forest and found his own supper, and no one ever knew what it was, for he didn't mention it. And the Scarecrow found a tree full of nuts[13] and filled Dorothy's basket with them, so that she would not be hungry for a long time.

She thought this was very kind and thoughtful of the Scarecrow, but she laughed heartily at the awkward way in which the poor creature picked up the nuts. His padded hands were so clumsy and the nuts were so small that he dropped almost as many as he put in the basket. But the Scarecrow did not mind how long it took him to fill the basket, for it enabled him to keep away from the fire, as he feared a spark might get into his straw and burn him up. So he kept a good distance away from the flames, and only came near to cover Dorothy with dry leaves when she lay down to sleep. These kept her very snug and warm and she slept soundly until morning.

When it was daylight the girl bathed her face in a little rippling brook and soon after they all started toward the Emerald City.

This was to be an eventful day for the travellers. They had hardly been walking an hour when they saw before them a great ditch that crossed the road and divided the forest as far as they could see on either side. It was a very wide ditch, and when they crept up to the edge and looked into it they could see it was also very deep, and there were many big, jagged rocks at the bottom. The sides were so steep that none of them could climb down, and for a moment it seemed that their journey must end.

"What shall we do?" asked Dorothy, despairingly.

"I haven't the faintest idea," said the Tin Woodman; and the Lion shook his shaggy mane and looked thoughtful. But the Scarecrow said:

"We cannot fly, that is certain; neither can we climb down into this great ditch. Therefore, if we cannot jump over it, we must stop where we are."

"I think I could jump over it," said the Cowardly Lion, after measuring the distance carefully in his mind.

"Then we are all right," answered the Scarecrow, "for you can carry us all over on your back, one at a time."

"Well, I'll try it," said the Lion. "Who will go first?"

"I will," declared the Scarecrow; "for, if you found that you could not jump over the gulf, Dorothy would be killed, or the Tin Woodman badly dented on the rocks below. But if I am on your back it will not matter so much, for the fall would not hurt me at all."

"I am terribly afraid of falling, myself," said the Cowardly Lion, "but I suppose there is nothing to do but try it. So get on my back and we will make the attempt."

The Scarecrow sat upon the Lion's back, and the big beast walked to the edge of the gulf and crouched down.

"Why don't you run and jump?" asked the Scarecrow.

"Because that isn't the way we Lions do these things," he replied. Then giving a great spring, he shot through the air and landed safely on the other side. They were all greatly pleased to see how easily he did it, and after the Scarecrow had got down from his back the Lion sprang across the ditch again.

Dorothy thought she would go next; so she took Toto in her arms and climbed on the Lion's back, holding tightly to his mane with one hand. The next moment it seemed as if she was flying through the air; and then, before she had time to think about it, she was safe on the other side. The Lion went back a third time and got the Tin Woodman, and then they all sat down for a few moments to give the beast a chance to rest, for his great leaps had made his breath short, and he panted like a big dog that has been running too long.

They found the forest very thick on this side, and it looked dark and gloomy. After the Lion had rested they started along the road of yellow brick, silently wondering, each in his own mind, if ever they would come to the end of the woods and reach the bright sunshine again. To add to their discomfort, they soon heard strange noises in the depths of the forest, and the Lion whispered to them that it was in this part of the country that the Kalidahs lived.

"What are the Kalidahs?" asked the girl.

"They are monstrous beasts with bodies like bears and heads like tigers," replied the Lion; "and with claws so long and sharp that they could tear me in two as easily as I could kill Toto. I'm terribly afraid of the Kalidahs."

"I'm not surprised that you are," returned Dorothy. "They must be dreadful beasts."

The Lion was about to reply when suddenly they came to another gulf across the road; but this one was so broad and deep that the Lion knew at once he could not leap across it.

So they sat down to consider what they should do, and after serious thought the Scarecrow said,

"Here is a great tree, standing close to the ditch. If the Tin

Woodman can chop it down, so that it will fall to the other side, we can walk across it easily."

"That is a first rate idea," said the Lion. "One would almost suspect you had brains in your head, instead of straw."

The Woodman set to work at once, and so sharp was his axe that the tree was soon chopped nearly through. Then the Lion put his strong front legs against the tree and pushed with all his might, and slowly the big tree tipped and fell with a crash across the ditch, with its top branches on the other side.

They had just started to cross this queer bridge when a sharp growl made them all look up, and to their horror they saw running toward them two great beasts with bodies like bears and heads like tigers.

"They are the Kalidahs!"[14] said the Cowardly Lion, beginning to tremble.

"Quick!" cried the Scarecrow, "let us cross over."

So Dorothy went first, holding Toto in her arms; the Tin Woodman followed, and the Scarecrow came next. The Lion, although he was certainly afraid, turned to face the Kalidahs, and then he gave so loud and terrible a roar that Dorothy screamed and the Scarecrow fell over backwards, while even the fierce beasts stopped short and looked at him in surprise.

But, seeing they were bigger than the Lion, and remembering that there were two of them and only one of him, the Kalidahs again rushed forward, and the Lion crossed over the tree and turned to see what they would do next. Without stopping an instant the fierce beasts also began to cross the tree, and the Lion said to Dorothy,

"We are lost, for they will surely tear us to pieces with their sharp claws. But stand close behind me, and I will fight them as long as I am alive."

"Wait a minute!" called the Scarecrow. He had been thinking what was best to be done, and now he asked the Woodman to chop away the end of the tree that rested on their side of the ditch. The Tin Woodman began to use his axe at once, and, just as the two Kalidahs were nearly across, the tree fell with a crash into the gulf, carrying the ugly, snarling brutes with it, and both were dashed to pieces on the sharp rocks at the bottom.

"Well," said the Cowardly Lion, drawing a long breath of relief, "I see we are going to live a little while longer, and I am glad of it,

*"The tree fell with a crash into the gulf."*

for it must be a very uncomfortable thing not to be alive. Those creatures frightened me so badly that my heart is beating yet."

"Ah," said the Tin Woodman, sadly, "I wish I had a heart to beat."

This adventure made the travellers more anxious than ever to get out of the forest, and they walked so fast that Dorothy became tired, and had to ride on the Lion's back. To their great joy the trees became thinner the further they advanced, and in the afternoon they suddenly came upon a broad river, flowing swiftly just before them. On the other side of the water they could see the road of yellow brick running through a beautiful country, with green meadows dotted with bright flowers and all the road bordered with trees hanging full of delicious fruits. They were greatly pleased to see this delightful country before them.

"How shall we cross the river?" asked Dorothy.

"That is easily done," replied the Scarecrow. "The Tin Woodman must build us a raft, so we can float to the other side."

So the Woodman took his axe and began to chop down small trees to make a raft, and while he was busy at this the Scarecrow found on the river bank a tree full of fine fruit. This pleased Dorothy, who had eaten nothing but nuts all day, and she made a hearty meal of the ripe fruit.

But it takes time to make a raft, even when one is as industrious and untiring as the Tin Woodman, and when night came the work was not done. So they found a cozy place under the trees where they slept well until the morning; and Dorothy dreamed of the Emerald City, and of the good Wizard Oz, who would soon send her back to her own home again.

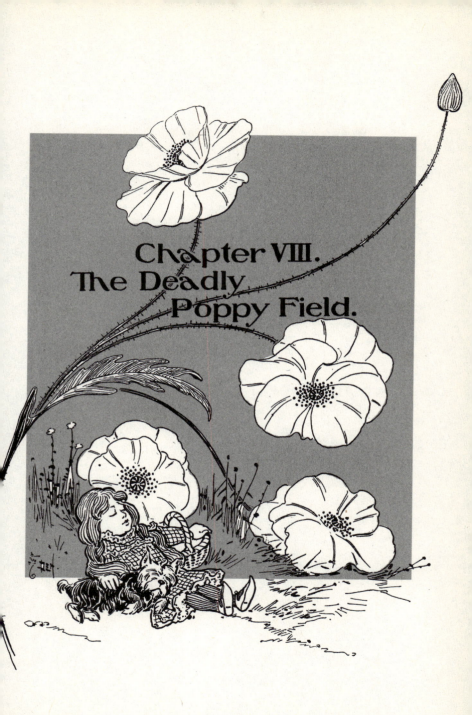

# Chapter VIII.
# The Deadly
# Poppy Field.

**O**vr little party of travellers awakened next morning refreshed and full of hope, and Dorothy breakfasted like a princess off peaches and plums from the trees beside the river.

Behind them was the dark forest they had passed safely through, although they had suffered many discouragements; but before them was a lovely, sunny country that seemed to beckon them on to the Emerald City.

To be sure, the broad river now cut them off from this beautiful land; but the raft was nearly done, and after the Tin Woodman had cut a few more logs and fastened them together with wooden pins, they were ready to start. Dorothy sat down in the middle of the raft and held Toto in her arms. When the Cowardly Lion stepped upon the raft it tipped badly, for he was big and heavy; but the Scarecrow and the Tin Woodman stood upon the other end to steady it, and they had long poles in their hands to push the raft through the water.

They got along quite well at first, but when they reached the middle of the river the swift current swept the raft down stream, farther and farther away from the road of yellow brick; and the water grew so deep that the long poles would not touch the bottom.

"This is bad," said the Tin Woodman, "for if we cannot get to the land we shall be carried into the country of the wicked Witch of the West, and she will enchant us and make us her slaves."

"And then I should get no brains," said the Scarecrow.

"And I should get no courage," said the Cowardly Lion.

"And I should get no heart," said the Tin Woodman.

"And I should never get back to Kansas," said Dorothy.

"We must certainly get to the Emerald City if we can," the Scarecrow continued, and he pushed so hard on his long pole that it stuck fast in the mud at the bottom of the river, and before he could pull it out again, or let go, the raft was swept away and the poor Scarecrow left clinging to the pole in the middle of the river.

"Good-bye!" he called after them, and they were very sorry to leave him; indeed, the Tin Woodman began to cry, but fortunately remembered that he might rust, and so dried his tears on Dorothy's apron.

Of course this was a bad thing for the Scarecrow.

"I am now worse off than when I first met Dorothy," he thought. "Then, I was stuck on a pole in a cornfield, where I could make believe scare the crows, at any rate; but surely there is no use for a Scarecrow stuck on a pole in the middle of a river. I am afraid I shall never have any brains, after all!"

Down the stream the raft floated, and the poor Scarecrow was left far behind. Then the Lion said:

"Something must be done to save us. I think I can swim to the shore and pull the raft after me, if you will only hold fast to the tip of my tail."

So he sprang into the water and the Tin Woodman caught fast hold of his tail, when the Lion began to swim with all his might toward the shore. It was hard work, although he was so big; but by and by they were drawn out of the current, and then Dorothy took the Tin Woodman's long pole and helped push the raft to the land.

They were all tired out when they reached the shore at last and stepped off upon the pretty green grass, and they also knew that the stream had carried them a long way past the road of yellow brick that led to the Emerald City.

"What shall we do now?" asked the Tin Woodman, as the Lion lay down on the grass to let the sun dry him.

"We must get back to the road, in some way," said Dorothy.

"The best plan will be to walk along the river bank until we come to the road again," remarked the Lion.

So, when they were rested, Dorothy picked up her basket and they started along the grassy bank, back to the road from which the river had carried them. It was a lovely country, with plenty of flowers and fruit trees and sunshine to cheer them, and had they not felt so sorry for the poor Scarecrow they could have been very happy.

They walked along as fast as they could, Dorothy only stopping once to pick a beautiful flower; and after a time the Tin Woodman cried out,

"Look!"

Then they all looked at the river and saw the Scarecrow perched upon his pole in the middle of the water, looking very lonely and sad.

"What can we do to save him?" asked Dorothy.

The Lion and the Woodman both shook their heads, for they did not know. So they sat down upon the bank and gazed wistfully at the Scarecrow until a Stork flew by, which, seeing them, stopped to rest at the water's edge.

"Who are you, and where are you going?" asked the Stork.

"I am Dorothy," answered the girl; "and these are my friends, the Tin Woodman and the Cowardly Lion; and we are going to the Emerald City."

"This isn't the road," said the Stork, as she twisted her long neck and looked sharply at the queer party.

"I know it," returned Dorothy, "but we have lost the Scarecrow, and are wondering how we shall get him again."

"Where is he?" asked the Stork.

"Over there in the river," answered the girl.

"If he wasn't so big and heavy I would get him for you," remarked the Stork.

"He isn't heavy a bit," said Dorothy, eagerly, "for he is stuffed with straw; and if you will bring him back to us we shall thank you ever and ever so much."

"Well, I'll try," said the Stork; "but if I find he is too heavy to carry I shall have to drop him in the river again."

So the big bird flew into the air and over the water till she came to where the Scarecrow was perched upon his pole. Then the Stork with her great claws grabbed the Scarecrow by the arm and carried him up into the air and back to the bank, where Dorothy and the Lion and the Tin Woodman and Toto were sitting.

When the Scarecrow found himself among his friends again he was so happy that he hugged them all, even the Lion and Toto; and as they walked along he sang "Tol-de-ri-de-oh!" at every step, he felt so gay.

"I was afraid I should have to stay in the river forever," he said, "but the kind Stork saved me, and if I ever get any brains I shall find the Stork again and do it some kindness in return."

"That's all right," said the Stork, who was flying along beside them. "I always like to help anyone in trouble. But I must go now, for my babies are waiting in the nest for me. I hope you will find the Emerald City and that Oz will help you."

"Thank you," replied Dorothy, and then the kind Stork[15] flew into the air and was soon out of sight.

They walked along listening to the singing of the bright-colored birds and looking at the lovely flowers which now became so thick that the ground was carpeted with them. There were big yellow and white and blue and purple blossoms, besides great clusters of scarlet poppies, which were so brilliant in color they almost dazzled Dorothy's eyes.

"Aren't they beautiful?" the girl asked, as she breathed in the spicy scent of the flowers.

"I suppose so," answered the Scarecrow. "When I have brains I shall probably like them better."

"If I only had a heart I should love them," added the Tin Woodman.

"I always did like flowers," said the Lion; "they seem so helpless and frail. But there are none in the forest so bright as these."

They now came upon more and more of the big scarlet poppies,

*The Stork carried him up into the air.*

and fewer and fewer of the other flowers; and soon they found themselves in the midst of a great meadow of poppies. Now it is well known that when there are many of these flowers together their odor is so powerful that anyone who breathes it falls asleep, and if the sleeper is not carried away from the scent of the flowers he sleeps on and on forever. But Dorothy did not know this, nor could she get away from the bright red flowers that were everywhere about; so presently her eyes grew heavy and she felt she must sit down to rest and to sleep.

But the Tin Woodman would not let her do this.

"We must hurry and get back to the road of yellow brick before dark," he said; and the Scarecrow agreed with him. So they kept walking until Dorothy could stand no longer. Her eyes closed in spite of herself and she forgot where she was and fell among the poppies, fast asleep.

"What shall we do?" asked the Tin Woodman.

"If we leave her here she will die," said the Lion. "The smell of the flowers is killing us all. I myself can scarcely keep my eyes open and the dog is asleep already."

It was true; Toto had fallen down beside his little mistress. But the Scarecrow and the Tin Woodman, not being made of flesh, were not troubled by the scent of the flowers.

"Run fast," said the Scarecrow to the Lion, "and get out of this deadly flower-bed as soon as you can. We will bring the little girl with us, but if you should fall asleep you are too big to be carried."

So the Lion aroused himself and bounded forward as fast as he could go. In a moment he was out of sight.

"Let us make a chair with our hands, and carry her," said the Scarecrow. So they picked up Toto and put the dog in Dorothy's lap, and then they made a chair with their hands for the seat and their arms for the arms and carried the sleeping girl between them through the flowers.

On and on they walked, and it seemed that the great carpet of deadly flowers that surrounded them would never end. They followed the bend of the river, and at last came upon their friend the Lion, lying fast asleep among the poppies.[16] The flowers had been too strong for the huge beast and he had given up, at last, and fallen only a short distance from the end of the poppybed, where the sweet grass spread in beautiful green fields before them.

"We can do nothing for him," said the Tin Woodman, sadly; "for he is much too heavy to lift. We must leave him here to sleep on forever, and perhaps he will dream that he has found courage at last."

"I'm sorry," said the Scarecrow; "the Lion was a very good comrade for one so cowardly. But let us go on."

They carried the sleeping girl to a pretty spot beside the river, far enough from the poppy field to prevent her breathing any more of the poison of the flowers, and here they laid her gently on the soft grass and waited for the fresh breeze to waken her.

# Chapter IX.
## The Queen of the Field Mice.

"**We** cannot be far from the road of yellow brick, now," remarked the Scarecrow, as he stood beside the girl, "for we have come nearly as far as the river carried us away."

The Tin Woodman was about to reply when he heard a low growl, and turning his head (which worked beautifully on hinges) he saw a strange beast come bounding over the grass towards them. It was, indeed, a great, yellow wildcat, and the Woodman thought it must be chasing something, for its ears were lying close to its head and its mouth was wide open, showing two rows of ugly teeth, while its red eyes glowed like balls of fire. As it came nearer the Tin Woodman saw that running before the beast was a little gray field-mouse, and although he had no heart he knew it was wrong for the wildcat to try to kill such a pretty, harmless creature.

So the Woodman raised his axe, and as the wildcat ran by he gave it a quick blow that cut the beast's head clean off from its body, and it rolled over at his feet in two pieces.

The field-mouse, now that it was freed from its enemy, stopped short; and coming slowly up to the Woodman it said, in a squeaky little voice,

"Oh, thank you! Thank you ever so much for saving my life."

"Don't speak of it, I beg of you," replied the Woodman. "I have no heart, you know, so I am careful to help all those who may need a friend, even if it happens to be only a mouse."

"Only a mouse!" cried the little animal, indignantly; "why, I am a Queen—the Queen of all the field-mice!"

"Oh, indeed," said the Woodman, making a bow.

"Therefore you have done a great deed, as well as a brave one, in saving my life," added the Queen.

At that moment several mice were seen running up as fast as their little legs could carry them, and when they saw their Queen they exclaimed,

"Oh, your Majesty, we thought you would be killed! How did you manage to escape the great Wildcat?" and they all bowed so low to the little Queen that they almost stood upon their heads.

"This funny tin man," she answered, "killed the Wildcat and saved my life. So hereafter you must all serve him, and obey his slightest wish."[17]

"We will!" cried all the mice, in a shrill chorus. And then they scampered in all directions, for Toto had awakened from his sleep, and seeing all these mice around him he gave one bark of delight and jumped right into the middle of the group. Toto had always loved to chase mice when he lived in Kansas, and he saw no harm in it.

But the Tin Woodman caught the dog in his arms and held him tight, while he called to the mice: "Come back! come back! Toto shall not hurt you."

At this the Queen of the Mice stuck her head out from a clump of grass and asked, in a timid voice,

"Are you sure he will not bite us?"

"I will not let him," said the Woodman; "so do not be afraid."

One by one the mice came creeping back, and Toto did not bark again, although he tried to get out of the Woodman's arms, and would have bitten him had he not known very well he was made of tin. Finally one of the biggest mice spoke.

"Is there anything we can do," it asked, "to repay you for saving the life of our Queen?"

"Nothing that I know of," answered the Woodman; but the Scarecrow, who had been trying to think, but could not because his head was stuffed with straw, said, quickly,

"Oh, yes; you can save our friend, the Cowardly Lion, who is asleep in the poppy bed."

"A Lion!" cried the little Queen; "why, he would eat us all up."

"Oh, no;" declared the Scarecrow; "this Lion is a coward."

"Really?" asked the Mouse.

"He says so himself," answered the Scarecrow, "and he would never hurt anyone who is our friend. If you will help us to save him I promise that he shall treat you all with kindness."

"Very well," said the Queen, "we will trust you. But what shall we do?"

"Are there many of these mice which call you Queen and are willing to obey you?"

"Oh, yes; there are thousands," she replied.

"Then send for them all to come here as soon as possible, and let each one bring a long piece of string."

The Queen turned to the mice that attended her and told them to go at once and get all her people. As soon as they heard her orders they ran away in every direction as fast as possible.

"Now," said the Scarecrow to the Tin Woodman, "you must go to those trees by the river-side and make a truck that will carry the Lion."

So the Woodman went at once to the trees and began to work; and he soon made a truck out of the limbs of trees, from which he chopped away all the leaves and branches. He fastened it together with wooden pegs and made the four wheels out of short pieces of a big tree trunk. So fast and so well did he work that by the time the mice began to arrive the truck was all ready for them.

They came from all directions, and there were thousands of them: big mice and little mice and middle-sized mice; and each one brought a piece of string in his mouth. It was about this time that Dorothy woke from her long sleep and opened her eyes. She was greatly astonished to find herself lying upon the grass, with thousands of mice standing around and looking at her timidly. But the Scarecrow told her about everything, and turning to the dignified little Mouse, he said,

"Permit me to introduce to you her Majesty, the Queen."

Dorothy nodded gravely and the Queen made a courtesy,* after which she became quite friendly with the little girl.

The Scarecrow and the Woodman now began to fasten the mice to the truck, using the strings they had brought. One end of a string was tied around the neck of each mouse and the other end to the truck. Of course the truck was a thousand times bigger than any of the mice who were to draw it; but when all the mice had been harnessed they were able to pull it quite easily. Even the Scarecrow and the Tin Woodman could sit on it, and were drawn swiftly by their queer little horses to the place where the Lion lay asleep.

After a great deal of hard work, for the Lion was heavy, they managed to get him up on the truck. Then the Queen hurriedly gave her people the order to start, for she feared if the mice stayed among the poppies too long they also would fall asleep.

At first the little creatures, many though they were, could hardly stir the heavily loaded truck; but the Woodman and the Scarecrow both pushed from behind, and they got along better. Soon they rolled the Lion out of the poppy bed to the green fields, where he could breathe the sweet, fresh air again, instead of the poisonous scent of the flowers.

Dorothy came to meet them and thanked the little mice warmly for saving her companion from death. She had grown so fond of the big Lion she was glad he had been rescued.

Then the mice were unharnessed from the truck and scampered away through the grass to their homes. The Queen of the Mice was the last to leave.

"If ever you need us again," she said, "come out into the field and call, and we shall hear you and come to your assistance. Good-bye!"

"Good-bye!" they all answered, and away the Queen ran, while Dorothy held Toto tightly lest he should run after her and frighten her.

After this they sat down beside the Lion until he should awaken; and the Scarecrow brought Dorothy some fruit from a tree near by, which she ate for her dinner.

---

*A curtsey.

*"Permit me to introduce to you her Majesty, the Queen."*

# Chapter X.
# The Guardian
## of the Gates.

**I**t was some time before the Cowardly Lion awakened, for he had lain among the poppies a long while, breathing in their deadly fragrance; but when he did open his eyes and roll off the truck he was very glad to find himself still alive.

"I ran as fast as I could," he said, sitting down and yawning; "but the flowers were too strong for me. How did you get me out?"

Then they told him of the field-mice, and how they had generously saved him from death; and the Cowardly Lion laughed, and said,

"I have always thought myself very big and terrible; yet such small things as flowers came near to killing me, and such small animals as mice have saved my life. How strange it all is! But, comrades, what shall we do now?"

"We must journey on until we find the road of yellow brick again," said Dorothy; "and then we can keep on to the Emerald City."

So, the Lion being fully refreshed, and feeling quite himself again, they all started upon the journey, greatly enjoying the walk through the soft, fresh grass; and it was not long before they reached the road of yellow brick and turned again toward the Emerald City where the great Oz dwelt.

The road was smooth and well paved, now, and the country about was beautiful; so that the travellers rejoiced in leaving the forest far behind, and with it the many dangers they had met in its gloomy shades. Once more they could see fences built beside the road; but these were painted green, and when they came to a small house, in which a farmer evidently lived, that also was painted green. They passed by several of these houses during the afternoon, and sometimes people came to the doors and looked at them as if they would like to ask questions; but no one came near them nor spoke to them because of the great Lion, of which they were much afraid. The people were all dressed in clothing of a lovely emerald green color and wore peaked hats like those of the Munchkins.

"This must be the Land of Oz," said Dorothy, "and we are surely getting near the Emerald City."

"Yes," answered the Scarecrow; "everything is green here,[18] while in the country of the Munchkins blue was the favorite color. But the people do not seem to be as friendly as the Munchkins and I'm afraid we shall be unable to find a place to pass the night."

"I should like something to eat besides fruit," said the girl, "and I'm sure Toto is nearly starved. Let us stop at the next house and talk to the people."

So, when they came to a good-sized farm house, Dorothy walked boldly up to the door and knocked. A woman opened it just far enough to look out, and said,

"What do you want, child, and why is that great Lion with you?"

"We wish to pass the night with you, if you will allow us," answered Dorothy; "and the Lion is my friend and comrade, and would not hurt you for the world."

"Is he tame?" asked the woman, opening the door a little wider.

"Oh, yes;" said the girl, "and he is a great coward, too; so that he will be more afraid of you than you are of him."

"Well," said the woman, after thinking it over and taking another peep at the Lion, "if that is the case you may come in, and I will give you some supper and a place to sleep."

So they all entered the house, where there were, besides the woman, two children and a man. The man had hurt his leg, and was lying on the couch in a corner. They seemed greatly surprised to see so strange a company, and while the woman was busy laying the table the man asked,

"Where are you all going?"

"To the Emerald City," said Dorothy, "to see the Great Oz."

"Oh, indeed!" exclaimed the man. "Are you sure that Oz will see you?"

"Why not?" she replied.

"Why, it is said that he never lets anyone come into his presence. I have been to the Emerald City many times, and it is a beautiful and wonderful place; but I have never been permitted to see the Great Oz, nor do I know of any living person who has seen him."

"Does he never go out?" asked the Scarecrow.

"Never. He sits day after day in the great throne room of his palace, and even those who wait upon him do not see him face to face."

"What is he like?" asked the girl.

"That is hard to tell," said the man, thoughtfully. "You see, Oz is a great Wizard, and can take on any form he wishes. So that some say he looks like a bird; and some say he looks like an elephant; and some say he looks like a cat. To others he appears as a beautiful fairy, or a brownie,[19] or in any other form that pleases him. But who the real Oz is, when he is in his own form, no living person can tell."

"That is very strange," said Dorothy; "but we must try, in some way, to see him, or we shall have made our journey for nothing."

"Why do you wish to see the terrible Oz?" asked the man.

"I want him to give me some brains," said the Scarecrow, eagerly.

"Oh, Oz could do that easily enough," declared the man. "He has more brains than he needs."

"And I want him to give me a heart," said the Tin Woodman.

"That will not trouble him," continued the man, "for Oz has a large collection of hearts, of all sizes and shapes."

"And I want him to give me courage," said the Cowardly Lion.

"Oz keeps a great pot of courage in his throne room," said the man, "which he has covered with a golden plate, to keep it from running over. He will be glad to give you some."

"And I want him to send me back to Kansas," said Dorothy.

"Where is Kansas?" asked the man, in surprise.

"I don't know," replied Dorothy, sorrowfully; "but it is my home, and I'm sure it's somewhere."

"Very likely. Well, Oz can do anything; so I suppose he will find Kansas for you. But first you must get to see him, and that will be a hard task; for the great Wizard does not like to see anyone, and he usually has his own way. But what do you want?" he continued, speaking to Toto. Toto only wagged his tail; for, strange to say, he could not speak.[20]

The woman now called to them that supper was ready, so they gathered around the table and Dorothy ate some delicious porridge and a dish of scrambled eggs and a plate of nice white bread, and enjoyed her meal. The Lion ate some of the porridge, but did not care for it, saying it was made from oats and oats were food for horses, not for lions. The Scarecrow and the Tin Woodman ate nothing at all. Toto ate a little of everything, and was glad to get a good supper again.

The woman now gave Dorothy a bed to sleep in, and Toto lay down beside her, while the Lion guarded the door of her room so she might not be disturbed. The Scarecrow and the Tin Woodman stood up in a corner and kept quiet all night, although of course they could not sleep.

The next morning, as soon as the sun was up, they started on their way, and soon saw a beautiful green glow in the sky just before them.

"That must be the Emerald City," said Dorothy.

As they walked on, the green glow became brighter and brighter, and it seemed that at last they were nearing the end of their travels. Yet it was afternoon before they came to the great wall that surrounded the City. It was high, and thick, and of a bright green color.

In front of them, and at the end of the road of yellow brick, was a big gate, all studded with emeralds that glittered so in the sun that even the painted eyes of the Scarecrow were dazzled by their brilliancy.

There was a bell beside the gate, and Dorothy pushed the button and heard a silvery tinkle sound within. Then the big gate swung slowly open, and they all passed through and found themselves in a high arched room, the walls of which glistened with countless emeralds.

*The Lion ate some of the porridge.*

Before them stood a little man about the same size as the Munchkins. He was clothed all in green, from his head to his feet, and even his skin was of a greenish tint. At his side was a large green box.

When he saw Dorothy and her companions the man asked,

"What do you wish in the Emerald City?"

"We came here to see the Great Oz," said Dorothy.

The man was so surprised at this answer that he sat down to think it over.

"It has been many years since anyone asked me to see Oz," he said, shaking his head in perplexity. "He is powerful and terrible, and if you come on an idle or foolish errand to bother the wise reflections of the Great Wizard, he might be angry and destroy you all in an instant."

"But it is not a foolish errand, nor an idle one," replied the Scarecrow; "it is important. And we have been told that Oz is a good Wizard."

"So he is," said the green man; "and he rules the Emerald City wisely and well. But to those who are not honest, or who approach him from curiosity, he is most terrible, and few have ever dared ask to see his face. I am the Guardian of the Gates, and since you demand to see the Great Oz I must take you to his palace. But first you must put on the spectacles."

"Why?" asked Dorothy.

"Because if you did not wear spectacles the brightness and glory of the Emerald City would blind you. Even those who live in the City must wear spectacles night and day. They are all locked on, for Oz so ordered it when the City was first built, and I have the only key that will unlock them."

He opened the big box, and Dorothy saw that it was filled with spectacles of every size and shape. All of them had green glasses in them. The Guardian of the Gates found a pair that would just fit Dorothy and put them over her eyes. There were two golden bands fastened to them that passed around the back of her head, where they were locked together by a little key that was at the end of a chain the Guardian of the Gates wore around his neck. When they were on, Dorothy could not take them off had she wished, but of course she did not want to be blinded by the glare of the Emerald City, so she said nothing.

Then the green man fitted spectacles for the Scarecrow and the Tin Woodman and the Lion, and even on little Toto; and all were locked fast with the key.

Then the Guardian of the Gates put on his own glasses and told them he was ready to show them to the Palace. Taking a big golden key from a peg on the wall he opened another gate, and they all followed him through the portal into the streets of the Emerald City.

# Chapter XI.
# The Wonderful
# Emerald City of OZ.

**E**ven with eyes protected
by the green specta-
cles Dorothy and her friends were at
first dazzled by the brilliancy of the wonderful City. The streets were lined with
beautiful houses all built of green marble
and studded everywhere with sparkling emeralds. They walked over a pavement of the same green
marble, and where the blocks were joined together were rows of
emeralds, set closely, and glittering in the brightness of the sun.
The window panes were of green glass; even the sky above the City
had a green tint, and the rays of the sun were green.

There were many people, men, women and children, walking
about, and these were all dressed in green clothes and had greenish skins. They looked at Dorothy and her strangely assorted company with wondering eyes, and the children all ran away and hid
behind their mothers when they saw the Lion; but no one spoke to
them. Many shops stood in the street, and Dorothy saw that everything in them was green. Green candy and green pop-corn were offered for sale, as well as green shoes, green hats and green clothes
of all sorts. At one place a man was selling green lemonade, and

when the children bought it Dorothy could see that they paid for it with green pennies.

There seemed to be no horses nor animals of any kind; the men carried things around in little green carts, which they pushed before them. Everyone seemed happy and contented and prosperous.

The Guardian of the Gates led them through the streets until they came to a big building, exactly in the middle of the City, which was the Palace of Oz, the Great Wizard. There was a soldier before the door, dressed in a green uniform and wearing a long green beard.

"Here are strangers," said the Guardian of the Gates to him, "and they demand to see the Great Oz."

"Step inside," answered the soldier, "and I will carry your message to him."

So they passed through the Palace gates and were led into a big room with a green carpet and lovely green furniture set with emeralds. The soldier made them all wipe their feet upon a green mat before entering this room, and when they were seated he said, politely,

"Please make yourselves comfortable while I go to the door of the Throne Room and tell Oz you are here."

They had to wait a long time before the soldier returned. When, at last, he came back, Dorothy asked,

"Have you seen Oz?"

"Oh, no;" returned the soldier; "I have never seen him. But I spoke to him as he sat behind his screen, and gave him your message. He says he will grant you an audience, if you so desire; but each one of you must enter his presence alone, and he will admit but one each day. Therefore, as you must remain in the Palace for several days, I will have you shown to rooms where you may rest in comfort after your journey."

"Thank you," replied the girl; "that is very kind of Oz."

The soldier now blew upon a green whistle, and at once a young girl, dressed in a pretty green silk gown, entered the room. She had lovely green hair and green eyes, and she bowed low before Dorothy as she said,

"Follow me and I will show you your room."

So Dorothy said good-bye to all her friends except Toto, and taking the dog in her arms followed the green girl through seven passages and up three flights of stairs[21] until they came to a room at the front of the Palace. It was the sweetest little room in the world, with a soft, comfortable bed that had sheets of green silk and a green velvet counterpane. There was a tiny fountain in the middle of the room, that shot a spray of green perfume into the air, to fall back into a beautifully carved green marble basin. Beautiful green flowers stood in the windows, and there was a shelf with a row of little green books. When Dorothy had time to open these books she found them full of queer green pictures that made her laugh, they were so funny.

In a wardrobe were many green dresses, made of silk and satin and velvet; and all of them fitted Dorothy exactly.

"Make yourself perfectly at home," said the green girl, "and if you wish for anything ring the bell. Oz will send for you to-morrow morning."

She left Dorothy alone and went back to the others. These she also led to rooms, and each one of them found himself lodged in a very pleasant part of the Palace. Of course this politeness was wasted on the Scarecrow; for when he found himself alone in his room he stood stupidly in one spot, just within the doorway, to wait till morning. It would not rest him to lie down, and he could not close his eyes; so he remained all night staring at a little spider which was weaving its web in a corner of the room, just as if it were not one of the most wonderful rooms in the world. The Tin Woodman lay down on his bed from force of habit, for he remembered when he was made of flesh; but not being able to sleep he passed the night moving his joints up and down to make sure they kept in good working order. The Lion would have preferred a bed of dried leaves in the forest, and did not like being shut up in a room; but he had too much sense to let this worry him, so he sprang upon the bed and rolled himself up like a cat and purred himself asleep in a minute.

The next morning, after breakfast, the green maiden came to fetch Dorothy, and she dressed her in one of the prettiest gowns[22] — made of green brocaded satin. Dorothy put on a green silk apron and tied a green ribbon around Toto's neck, and they started for the Throne Room of the Great Oz.

First they came to a great hall in which were many ladies and gentlemen of the court, all dressed in rich costumes. These people had nothing to do but talk to each other, but they always came to wait outside the Throne Room every morning, although they were never permitted to see Oz. As Dorothy entered they looked at her curiously, and one of them whispered,

"Are you really going to look upon the face of Oz the Terrible?"

"Of course," answered the girl, "if he will see me."

"Oh, he will see you," said the soldier who had taken her message to the Wizard, "although he does not like to have people ask to see him. Indeed, at first he was angry, and said I should send you back where you came from. Then he asked me what you looked like, and when I mentioned your silver shoes he was very much interested. At last I told him about the mark upon your forehead, and he decided he would admit you to his presence."

Just then a bell rang, and the green girl said to Dorothy,

"That is the signal. You must go into the Throne Room alone."

She opened a little door and Dorothy walked boldly through and found herself in a wonderful place. It was a big, round room with a high arched roof, and the walls and ceiling and floor were covered with large emeralds set closely together. In the center of the roof was a great light, as bright as the sun, which made the emeralds sparkle in a wonderful manner.

But what interested Dorothy most was the big throne of green marble that stood in the middle of the room. It was shaped like a chair and sparkled with gems, as did everything else. In the center of the chair was an enormous Head, without body to support it or any arms or legs whatever. There was no hair upon this head, but it had eyes and nose and mouth, and was bigger than the head of the biggest giant.

As Dorothy gazed upon this in wonder and fear the eyes turned slowly and looked at her sharply and steadily. Then the mouth moved, and Dorothy heard a voice say:

"I am Oz, the Great and Terrible. Who are you, and why do you seek me?"

It was not such an awful voice as she had expected to come from the big Head; so she took courage and answered,

"I am Dorothy, the Small and Meek.[23] I have come to you for help."

*The eyes looked at her thoughtfully.*

The eyes looked at her thoughtfully for a full minute. Then said the voice:

"Where did you get the silver shoes?"

"I got them from the wicked Witch of the East, when my house fell on her and killed her," she replied.

"Where did you get the mark upon your forehead?" continued the voice.

"That is where the good Witch of the North kissed me when she bade me good-bye and sent me to you," said the girl.

Again the eyes looked at her sharply, and they saw she was telling the truth. Then Oz asked,

"What do you wish me to do?"

"Send me back to Kansas, where my Aunt Em and Uncle Henry are," she answered, earnestly. "I don't like your country, although it is so beautiful. And I am sure Aunt Em will be dreadfully worried over my being away so long."

The eyes winked three times, and then they turned up to the ceiling and down to the floor and rolled around so queerly that they seemed to see every part of the room. And at last they looked at Dorothy again.

"Why should I do this for you?"[24] asked Oz.

"Because you are strong and I am weak; because you are a Great Wizard and I am only a helpless little girl," she answered.

"But you were strong enough to kill the wicked Witch of the East," said Oz.

"That just happened," returned Dorothy, simply; "I could not help it."

"Well," said the Head, "I will give you my answer. You have no right to expect me to send you back to Kansas unless you do something for me in return. In this country everyone must pay for everything he gets. If you wish me to use my magic power to send you home again you must do something for me first. Help me and I will help you."

"What must I do?" asked the girl.

"Kill the Wicked Witch of the West," answered Oz.

"But I cannot!" exclaimed Dorothy, greatly surprised.

"You killed the Witch of the East and you wear the silver shoes, which bear a powerful charm. There is now but one Wicked Witch left in all this land, and when you can tell me she is dead I will send you back to Kansas—but not before."

The little girl began to weep, she was so much disappointed; and the eyes winked again and looked upon her anxiously, as if the Great Oz felt that she could help him if she would.

"I never killed anything, willingly," she sobbed; "and even if I wanted to, how could I kill the Wicked Witch? If you, who are Great and Terrible, cannot kill her yourself, how do you expect me to do it?"

"I do not know," said the Head; "but that is my answer, and until the Wicked Witch dies you will not see your Uncle and Aunt again. Remember that the Witch is Wicked—tremendously Wicked— and ought to be killed. Now go, and do not ask to see me again until you have done your task."

Sorrowfully Dorothy left the Throne Room and went back where the Lion and the Scarecrow and the Tin Woodman were waiting to hear what Oz had said to her.

"There is no hope for me," she said, sadly, "for Oz will not send me home until I have killed the Wicked Witch of the West; and that I can never do."

Her friends were sorry, but could do nothing to help her; so she went to her own room and lay down on the bed and cried herself to sleep.

The next morning the soldier with the green whiskers came to the Scarecrow and said,

"Come with me, for Oz has sent for you."

So the Scarecrow followed him and was admitted into the great Throne Room, where he saw, sitting in the emerald throne, a most lovely lady. She was dressed in green silk gauze and wore upon her flowing green locks a crown of jewels. Growing from her shoulders were wings, gorgeous in color and so light that they fluttered if the slightest breath of air reached them.

When the Scarecrow had bowed, as prettily as his straw stuffing would let him, before this beautiful creature, she looked upon him sweetly, and said,

"I am Oz, the Great and Terrible. Who are you, and why do you seek me?"

Now the Scarecrow, who had expected to see the great Head

Dorothy had told him of, was much astonished; but he answered her bravely.

"I am only a Scarecrow, stuffed with straw. Therefore I have no brains, and I come to you praying that you will put brains in my head instead of straw, so that I may become as much a man as any other in your dominions."

"Why should I do this for you?" asked the Lady.

"Because you are wise and powerful, and no one else can help me," answered the Scarecrow.

"I never grant favors without some return," said Oz; "but this much I will promise. If you will kill for me the Wicked Witch of the West I will bestow upon you a great many brains, and such good brains that you will be the wisest man in all the Land of Oz."

"I thought you asked Dorothy to kill the Witch," said the Scarecrow, in surprise.

"So I did. I don't care who kills her. But until she is dead I will not grant your wish. Now go, and do not seek me again until you have earned the brains you so greatly desire."

The Scarecrow went sorrowfully back to his friends and told them what Oz had said; and Dorothy was surprised to find that the great Wizard was not a Head, as she had seen him, but a lovely Lady.

"All the same," said the Scarecrow, "she needs a heart as much as the Tin Woodman."[25]

On the next morning the soldier with the green whiskers came to the Tin Woodman and said,

"Oz has sent for you. Follow me,"

So the Tin Woodman followed him and came to the great Throne Room. He did not know whether he would find Oz a lovely Lady or a Head, but he hoped it would be the lovely lady. "For," he said to himself, "if it is the Head, I am sure I shall not be given a heart, since a head has no heart of its own and therefore cannot feel for me. But if it is the lovely Lady I shall beg hard for a heart, for all ladies are themselves said to be kindly hearted."

But when the Woodman entered the great Throne Room he saw neither the Head nor the Lady, for Oz had taken the shape of a most terrible Beast. It was nearly as big as an elephant, and the green throne seemed hardly strong enough to hold its weight. The

Beast had a head like that of a rhinoceros, only there were five eyes in its face. There were five long arms growing out of its body and it also had five long, slim legs. Thick, woolly hair covered every part of it, and a more dreadful looking monster could not be imagined. It was fortunate the Tin Woodman had no heart at that moment, for it would have beat loud and fast from terror. But being only tin, the Woodman was not at all afraid, although he was much disappointed.

"I am Oz, the Great and Terrible," spake the Beast, in a voice that was one great roar. "Who are you, and why do you seek me?"

"I am a Woodman, and made of tin. Therefore I have no heart, and cannot love. I pray you to give me a heart that I may be as other men are."

"Why should I do this?" demanded the Beast.

"Because I ask it, and you alone can grant my request," answered the Woodman.

Oz gave a low growl at this, but said, gruffly,

"If you indeed desire a heart, you must earn it."

"How?" asked the Woodman.

"Help Dorothy to kill the Wicked Witch of the West," replied the Beast. "When the Witch is dead, come to me, and I will then give you the biggest and kindest and most loving heart in all the Land of Oz."

So the Tin Woodman was forced to return sorrowfully to his friends and tell them of the terrible Beast he had seen. They all wondered greatly at the many forms the great Wizard could take upon himself, and the Lion said,

"If he is a Beast when I go to see him, I shall roar my loudest, and so frighten him that he will grant all I ask. And if he is the lovely Lady, I shall pretend to spring upon her, and so compel her to do my bidding. And if he is the great Head, he will be at my mercy; for I will roll this head all about the room until he promises to give us what we desire. So be of good cheer my friends, for all will yet be well."

The next morning the soldier with the green whiskers led the Lion to the great Throne Room and bade him enter the presence of Oz.

The Lion at once passed through the door, and glancing around saw, to his surprise, that before the throne was a Ball of Fire, so fierce and glowing he could scarcely bear to gaze upon it. His first thought was that Oz had by accident caught on fire and was burning up; but, when he tried to go nearer, the heat was so intense that it singed his whiskers, and he crept back tremblingly to a spot nearer the door.

Then a low, quiet voice came from the Ball of Fire, and these were the words it spoke:

"I am Oz, the Great and Terrible. Who are you, and why do you seek me?" And the Lion answered,

"I am a Cowardly Lion, afraid of everything. I come to you to beg that you give me courage, so that in reality I may become the King of Beasts, as men call me."

"Why should I give you courage?" demanded Oz.

"Because of all Wizards you are the greatest, and alone have power to grant my request," answered the Lion.

The Ball of Fire burned fiercely for a time, and the voice said,

"Bring me proof that the Wicked Witch is dead, and that moment I will give you courage. But so long as the Witch lives you must remain a coward."

The Lion was angry at this speech, but could say nothing in reply, and while he stood silently gazing at the Ball of Fire it became so furiously hot that he turned tail and rushed from the room. He was glad to find his friends waiting for him, and told them of his terrible interview with the Wizard.

"What shall we do now?" asked Dorothy, sadly.

"There is only one thing we can do," returned the Lion, "and that is to go to the land of the Winkies, seek out the Wicked Witch, and destroy her."

"But suppose we cannot?" said the girl.

"Then I shall never have courage," declared the Lion.

"And I shall never have brains," added the Scarecrow.

"And I shall never have a heart," spoke the Tin Woodman.

"And I shall never see Aunt Em and Uncle Henry," said Dorothy, beginning to cry.

"Be careful!" cried the green girl, "the tears will fall on your green silk gown, and spot it."

So Dorothy dried her eyes and said,

"I suppose we must try it; but I am sure I do not want to kill anybody, even to see Aunt Em again."

"I will go with you: but I'm too much of a coward to kill the Witch," said the Lion.

"I will go too," declared the Scarecrow: "but I shall not be of much help to you, I am such a fool."

"I haven't the heart to harm even a Witch," remarked the Tin Woodman; "but if you go I certainly shall go with you."

Therefore it was decided to start upon their journey the next morning, and the Woodman sharpened his axe on a green grindstone and had all his joints properly oiled. The Scarecrow stuffed himself with fresh straw and Dorothy put new paint on his eyes that he might see better. The green girl, who was very kind to them, filled Dorothy's basket with good things to eat, and fastened a little bell around Toto's neck with a green ribbon.

They went to bed quite early and slept soundly until daylight, when they were awakened by the crowing of a green cock that lived in the back yard of the Palace, and the cackling of a hen that had laid a green egg.

Chapter XII.
The Search for the
Wicked Witch

**The** soldier with the green whiskers led them through the streets of the Emerald City until they reached the room where the Guardian of the Gates lived. This officer unlocked their spectacles[26] to put them back in his great box, and then he politely opened the gate for our friends.

"Which road leads to the Wicked Witch of the West?" asked Dorothy.

"There is no road," answered the Guardian of the Gates; "no one ever wishes to go that way."

"How, then, are we to find her?" enquired the girl.

"That will be easy," replied the man; "for when she knows you are in the Country of the Winkies she will find you, and make you all her slaves."

"Perhaps not," said the Scarecrow, "for we mean to destroy her."

"Oh, that is different," said the Guardian of the Gates. "No one has ever destroyed her before, so I naturally thought she would make slaves of you, as she has of all the rest. But take care; for she is wicked and fierce, and may not allow you to destroy her. Keep to the West, where the sun sets, and you cannot fail to find her."

*The soldier with the green whiskers led them through the streets.*

They thanked him and bade him good-bye, and turned toward the West, walking over fields of soft grass dotted here and there with daisies and buttercups. Dorothy still wore the pretty silk dress she had put on in the Palace, but now, to her surprise, she found it was no longer green, but pure white. The ribbon around Toto's neck had also lost its green color and was as white as Dorothy's dress.

The Emerald City was soon left far behind. As they advanced the ground became rougher and hillier, for there were no farms nor houses in this country of the West, and the ground was untilled.

In the afternoon the sun shone hot in their faces, for there were no trees to offer them shade; so that before night Dorothy and Toto and the Lion were tired, and lay down upon the grass and fell asleep, with the Woodman and the Scarecrow keeping watch.

Now the Wicked Witch of the West had but one eye, yet that was as powerful as a telescope, and could see everywhere. So, as she sat in the door of her castle, she happened to look around and saw Dorothy lying asleep, with her friends all about her. They were a long distance off, but the Wicked Witch was angry to find them in her country; so she blew upon a silver whistle that hung around her neck.

At once there came running to her from all directions a pack of great wolves. They had long legs and fierce eyes and sharp teeth.

"Go to those people," said the Witch, "and tear them to pieces."

"Are you not going to make them your slaves?" asked the leader of the wolves.

"No," she answered, "one is of tin, and one of straw; one is a girl and another a lion. None of them is fit to work, so you may tear them into small pieces."

"Very well," said the wolf, and he dashed away at full speed, followed by the others.

It was lucky the Scarecrow and the Woodman were wide awake and heard the wolves coming.

"This is my fight," said the Woodman; "so get behind me and I will meet them as they come."

He seized his axe,[27] which he had made very sharp, and as the leader of the wolves came on the Tin Woodman swung his arm and chopped the wolf's head from its body, so that it immediately died. As soon as he could raise his axe another wolf came up, and he also fell under the sharp edge of the Tin Woodman's weapon. There were forty wolves, and forty times a wolf was killed; so that at last they all lay dead in a heap before the Woodman.

Then he put down his axe and sat beside the Scarecrow, who said,

"It was a good fight, friend."

They waited until Dorothy awoke the next morning. The little girl was quite frightened when she saw the great pile of shaggy wolves, but the Tin Woodman told her all. She thanked him for saving them and sat down to breakfast, after which they started again upon their journey.

Now this same morning the Wicked Witch came to the door of her castle and looked out with her one eye that could see afar off. She saw all her wolves lying dead, and the strangers still travelling through her country. This made her angrier than before, and she blew her silver whistle twice.

Straightway a great flock of wild crows came flying toward her, enough to darken the sky. And the Wicked Witch said to the King Crow,

"Fly at once to the strangers; peck out their eyes and tear them to pieces."

The wild crows flew in one great flock toward Dorothy and her companions. When the little girl saw them coming she was afraid. But the Scarecrow said,

"This is my battle;[28] so lie down beside me and you will not be harmed."

So they all lay upon the ground except the Scarecrow, and he stood up and stretched out his arms. And when the crows saw him they were frightened, as these birds always are by scarecrows, and did not dare to come any nearer. But the King Crow said,

"It is only a stuffed man. I will peck his eyes out."

The King Crow flew at the Scarecrow, who caught it by the head and twisted its neck until it died. And then another crow flew at him, and the Scarecrow twisted its neck also. There were forty crows, and forty times the Scarecrow twisted a neck, until at last all were lying dead beside him. Then he called to his companions to rise, and again they went upon their journey.

When the Wicked Witch looked out again and saw all her crows lying in a heap, she got into a terrible rage, and blew three times upon her silver whistle.

Forthwith there was heard a great buzzing in the air, and a swarm of black bees came flying towards her.

"Go to the strangers and sting them to death!" commanded the Witch, and the bees turned and flew rapidly until they came to where Dorothy and her friends were walking. But the Woodman had seen them coming and the Scarecrow had decided what to do.

"Take out my straw and scatter it over the little girl and the dog and the lion," he said to the Woodman, "and the bees cannot sting them." This the Woodman did, and as Dorothy lay close beside the Lion and held Toto in her arms, the straw covered them entirely.

The bees came and found no one but the Woodman to sting, so they flew at him and broke off all their stings against the tin, without hurting the Woodman at all. And as bees cannot live when their stings are broken that was the end of the black bees, and they lay scattered thick about the Woodman, like little heaps of fine coal.

Then Dorothy and the Lion got up, and the girl helped the Tin Woodman put the straw back into the Scarecrow again, until he was as good as ever. So they started upon their journey once more.

The Wicked Witch was so angry when she saw her black bees in little heaps like fine coal that she stamped her foot and tore her hair and gnashed her teeth. And then she called a dozen of her slaves, who were the Winkies, and gave them sharp spears, telling them to go to the strangers and destroy them.

The Winkies were not a brave people, but they had to do as they were told; so they marched away until they came near to Dorothy. Then the Lion gave a great roar and sprang toward them, and the poor Winkies were so frightened that they ran back as fast as they could.

When they returned to the castle the Wicked Witch beat them well with a strap, and sent them back to their work, after which she sat down to think what she should do next. She could not understand how all her plans to destroy these strangers had failed; but she was a powerful Witch, as well as a wicked one, and she soon made up her mind how to act.

There was, in her cupboard, a Golden Cap, with a circle of diamonds and rubies running round it. This Golden Cap had a charm.

Whoever owned it could call three times upon the Winged Monkeys, who would obey any order they were given. But no person could command these strange creatures more than three times. Twice already the Wicked Witch had used the charm of the Cap. Once was when she had made the Winkies her slaves, and set herself to rule over their country. The Winged Monkeys had helped her do this. The second time was when she had fought against the Great Oz himself, and driven him out of the land of the West. The Winged Monkeys had also helped her in doing this. Only once more could she use this Golden Cap, for which reason she did not like to do so until all her other powers were exhausted. But now that her fierce wolves and her wild crows and her stinging bees were gone, and her slaves had been scared away by the Cowardly Lion, she saw there was only one way left to destroy Dorothy and her friends.

So the Wicked Witch took the Golden Cap from her cupboard and placed it upon her head. Then she stood upon her left foot and said, slowly,

"Ep-pe, pep-pe, kak-ke!"

Next she stood upon her right foot and said,

"Hil-lo, hol-lo, hel-lo!"

After this she stood upon both feet and cried in a loud voice,

"Ziz-zy, zuz-zy, zik!"

Now the charm began to work. The sky was darkened, and a low rumbling sound was heard in the air. There was a rushing of many wings; a great chattering and laughing; and the sun came out of the dark sky to show the Wicked Witch surrounded by a crowd of monkeys, each with a pair of immense and powerful wings on his shoulders.

One, much bigger than the others, seemed to be their leader. He flew close to the Witch and said,

"You have called us for the third and last time. What do you command?"

"Go to the strangers who are within my land and destroy them all except the Lion," said the Wicked Witch. "Bring that beast to me, for I have a mind to harness him like a horse, and make him work."

"Your commands shall be obeyed," said the leader; and then,

with a great deal of chattering and noise, the Winged Monkeys flew away to the place where Dorothy and her friends were walking.

Some of the Monkeys seized the Tin Woodman and carried him through the air until they were over a country thickly covered with sharp rocks. Here they dropped the poor Woodman, who fell a great distance to the rocks, where he lay so battered and dented that he could neither move nor groan.

Others of the Monkeys caught the Scarecrow, and with their long fingers pulled all of the straw out of his clothes and head. They made his hat and boots and clothes into a small bundle and threw it into the top branches of a tall tree.

The remaining Monkeys threw pieces of stout rope around the Lion and wound many coils about his body and head and legs, until he was unable to bite or scratch or struggle in any way. Then they lifted him up and flew away with him to the Witch's castle, where he was placed in a small yard with a high iron fence around it, so that he could not escape.

But Dorothy they did not harm at all. She stood, with Toto in her arms, watching the sad fate of her comrades and thinking it would soon be her turn. The leader of the Winged Monkeys flew up to her, his long, hairy arms stretched out and his ugly face grinning terriby; but he saw the mark of the good Witch's kiss upon her forehead and stopped short, motioning the others not to touch her.

"We dare not harm this little girl," he said to them, "for she is protected by the Power of Good, and that is greater than the Power of Evil.[29] All we can do is to carry her to the castle of the Wicked Witch and leave her there."

So, carefully and gently, they lifted Dorothy in their arms and carried her swiftly through the air until they came to the castle, where they set her down upon the front door step. Then the leader said to the Witch,

"We have obeyed you as far as we were able. The Tin Woodman and the Scarecrow are destroyed, and the Lion is tied up in your yard. The little girl we dare not harm, nor the dog she carries in her arms. Your power over our band is now ended, and you will never see us again."

Then all the Winged Monkeys, with much laughing and chattering and noise, flew into the air and were soon out of sight.

*The Monkeys wound many coils about his body.*

The Wicked Witch was both surprised and worried when she saw the mark on Dorothy's forehead, for she knew well that neither the Winged Monkeys nor she, herself, dare hurt the girl in any way. She looked down at Dorothy's feet, and seeing the Silver Shoes, began to tremble with fear, for she knew what a powerful charm belonged to them. At first the Witch was tempted to run away from Dorothy; but she happened to look into the child's eyes and saw how simple the soul behind them was, and that the little girl did not know of the wonderful power the Silver Shoes gave her. So the Wicked Witch laughed to herself, and thought, "I can still make her my slave, for she does not know how to use her power." Then she said to Dorothy, harshly and severely,

"Come with me; and see that you mind everything I tell you, for if you do not I will make an end of you, as I did of the Tin Woodman and the Scarecrow."

Dorothy followed her through many of the beautiful rooms in her castle until they came to the kitchen, where the Witch bade her clean the pots and kettles and sweep the floor and keep the fire fed with wood.

Dorothy went to work meekly, with her mind made up to work as hard as she could; for she was glad the Wicked Witch had decided not to kill her.

With Dorothy hard at work the Witch thought she would go into the court-yard and harness the Cowardly Lion like a horse; it would amuse her, she was sure, to make him draw her chariot whenever she wished to go to drive. But as she opened the gate the Lion gave a loud roar and bounded at her so fiercely that the Witch was afraid, and ran out and shut the gate again.

"If I cannot harness you," said the Witch to the Lion, speaking through the bars of the gate, "I can starve you. You shall have nothing to eat until you do as I wish."

So after that she took no food to the imprisoned Lion; but every day she came to the gate at noon and asked,

"Are you ready to be harnessed like a horse?"

And the Lion would answer,

"No. If you come in this yard I will bite you."

The reason the Lion did not have to do as the Witch wished was that every night, while the woman was asleep, Dorothy carried him food from the cupboard. After he had eaten he would lie down on his bed of straw, and Dorothy would lie beside him and put her head on his soft, shaggy mane, while they talked of their troubles and tried to plan some way to escape. But they could find no way to get out of the castle, for it was constantly guarded by the yellow Winkies, who were the slaves of the Wicked Witch and too afraid of her not to do as she told them.

The girl had to work hard during the day, and often the Witch threatened to beat her with the same old umbrella she always carried in her hand. But, in truth, she did not dare to strike Dorothy, because of the mark upon her forehead. The child did not know this, and was full of fear for herself and Toto. Once the Witch struck Toto a blow with her umbrella and the brave little dog flew at her and bit her leg, in return. The Witch did not bleed where she was bitten, for she was so wicked that the bood in her had dried up many years before.

Dorothy's life became very sad as she grew to understand that it would be harder than ever to get back to Kansas and Aunt Em again. Sometimes she would cry bitterly for hours, with Toto sitting at her feet and looking into her face, whining dismally to show how sorry he was for his little mistress. Toto did not really care whether he was in Kansas or the Land of Oz so long as Dorothy was with him; but he knew the little girl was unhappy, and that made him unhappy too.

Now the Wicked Witch had a great longing to have for her own the Silver Shoes which the girl always wore. Her Bees and her Crows and her Wolves were lying in heaps and drying up, and she had used up all the power of the Golden Cap; but if she could only get hold of the Silver Shoes they would give her more power than all the other things she had lost. She watched Dorothy carefully, to see if she ever took off her shoes, thinking she might steal them. But the child was so proud of her pretty shoes that she never took them off except at night and when she took her bath. The Witch was too much afraid of the dark to dare go in Dorothy's room at night to take the shoes, and her dread of water was greater than her fear of the dark, so she never came near when Dorothy was bathing. Indeed, the old Witch never touched water, nor ever let water touch her in any way.

But the wicked creature was very cunning, and she finally thought of a trick that would give her what she wanted. She placed a bar of iron in the middle of the kitchen floor, and then by her magic arts made the iron invisible to human eyes. So that when Dorothy walked across the floor she stumbled over the bar, not being able to see it, and fell at full length. She was not much hurt, but in her fall one of the Silver Shoes came off, and before she could reach it the Witch had snatched it away and put it on her own skinny foot.

The wicked woman was greatly pleased with the success of her trick, for as long as she had one of the shoes she owned half the power of their charm, and Dorothy could not use it against her, even had she known how to do so.

The little girl, seeing she had lost one of her pretty shoes, grew angry, and said to the Witch,

"Give me back my shoe!"

"I will not," retorted the Witch, "for it is now my shoe, and not yours."

"You are a wicked creature!" cried Dorothy. "You have no right to take my shoe from me."

"I shall keep it, just the same," said the Witch, laughing at her, "and some day I shall get the other one from you, too."

This made Dorothy so very angry that she picked up the bucket of water that stood near and dashed it over the Witch, wetting her from head to foot.

Instantly the wicked woman gave a loud cry of fear; and then, as Dorothy looked at her in wonder, the Witch began to shrink and fall away.

"See what you have done!" she screamed. "In a minute I shall melt away."

"I'm very sorry, indeed," said Dorothy, who was truly frightened to see the Witch actually melting away like brown sugar before her very eyes.

"Didn't you know water would be the end of me?" asked the Witch, in a wailing, despairing voice.

"Of course not," answered Dorothy; "how should I?"

"Well, in a few minutes I shall be all melted, and you will have the castle to yourself. I have been wicked in my day, but I never thought a little girl like you would ever be able to melt me and end my wicked deeds. Look out—here I go!"

With these words the Witch fell down in a brown, melted, shapeless mass and began to spread over the clean boards of the kitchen floor. Seeing that she had really melted away to nothing, Dorothy drew another bucket of water and threw it over the mess. She then swept it all out the door. After picking out the silver shoe, which was all that was left of the old woman, she cleaned and dried it with a cloth, and put it on her foot again. Then, being at last free to do as she chose, she ran out to the court-yard to tell the Lion that the Wicked Witch of the West had come to an end, and that they were no longer prisoners in a strange land.[30]

# Chapter XIII.
# The Rescue

**The** Cowardly Lion was much pleased to hear that the Wicked Witch had been melted by a bucket of water, and Dorothy at once unlocked the gate of his prison and set him free. They went in together to the castle, where Dorothy's first act was to call all the Winkies together and tell them that they were no longer slaves.

There was great rejoicing among the yellow Winkies, for they had been made to work hard during many years for the Wicked Witch, who had always treated them with great cruelty. They kept this day as a holiday, then and ever after, and spent the time in feasting and dancing.

"If our friends, the Scarecrow and the Tin Woodman, were only with us," said the Lion, "I should be quite happy."

"Don't you suppose we could rescue them?" asked the girl, anxiously.

"We can try," answered the Lion.

So they called the yellow Winkies and asked them if they would help to rescue their friends, and the Winkies said that they would be delighted to do all in their power for Dorothy, who had set them free from bondage. So she chose a number of the Winkies who looked as if they knew the most, and they all started away. They travelled that day and part of the next until they came to the rocky plain where the Tin Woodman lay, all battered and bent. His axe was near him, but the blade was rusted and the handle broken off short.

The Winkies lifted him tenderly in their arms, and carried him back to the yellow castle again, Dorothy shedding a few tears by the way at the sad plight of her old friend, and the Lion looking sober and sorry. When they reached the castle Dorothy said to the Winkies,

"Are any of your people tinsmiths?"

"Oh, yes; some of us are very good tinsmiths," they told her.

"Then bring them to me," she said. And when the tinsmiths came, bringing with them all their tools in baskets, she enquired,

"Can you straighten out those dents in the Tin Woodman, and bend him back into shape again, and solder him together where he is broken?"

The tinsmiths looked the Woodman over carefully and then answered that they thought they could mend him so he would be as good as ever. So they set to work in one of the big yellow rooms of the castle and worked for three days and four nights, hammering and twisting and bending and soldering and polishing and pounding at the legs and body and head of the Tin Woodman, until at last he was straightened out into his old form, and his joints worked as well as ever. To be sure, there were several patches on him, but the tinsmiths did a good job, and as the Woodman was not a vain man he did not mind the patches at all.

When, at last, he walked into Dorothy's room and thanked her for rescuing him, he was so pleased that he wept tears of joy, and Dorothy had to wipe every tear carefully from his face with her apron, so his joints would not be rusted. At the same time her own tears fell thick and fast at the joy of meeting her old friend again, and these tears did not need to be wiped away. As for the Lion, he wiped his eyes so often with the tip of his tail that it became quite wet, and he was obliged to go out into the court-yard and hold it in the sun till it dried.

*The tinsmiths worked for three days and four nights.*

"If we only had the Scarecrow with us again," said the Tin Woodman, when Dorothy had finished telling him everything that had happened, "I should be quite happy."

"We must try to find him," said the girl.

So she called the Winkies to help her, and they walked all that day and part of the next until they came to the tall tree in the branches of which the Winged Monkeys had tossed the Scarecrow's clothes.

It was a very tall tree, and the trunk was so smooth that no one could climb it; but the Woodman said at once,

"I'll chop it down, and then we can get the Scarecrow's clothes."

Now while the tinsmiths had been at work mending the Woodman himself, another of the Winkies, who was a goldsmith, had made an axe-handle of solid gold and fitted it to the Woodman's axe, instead of the old broken handle. Others polished the blade until all the rust was removed and it glistened like burnished silver.

As soon as he had spoken, the Tin Woodman began to chop, and in a short time the tree fell over with a crash, when the Scarecrow's clothes fell out of the branches and rolled off on the ground.

Dorothy picked them up and had the Winkies carry them back to the castle, where they were stuffed with nice, clean straw; and, behold! here was the Scarecrow, as good as ever, thanking them over and over again for saving him.

Now they were reunited, Dorothy and her friends spent a few happy days at the Yellow Castle, where they found everything they needed to make them comfortable. But one day the girl thought of Aunt Em, and said,

"We must go back to Oz, and claim his promise."

"Yes," said the Woodman, "at last I shall get my heart."

"And I shall get my brains," added the Scarecrow, joyfully.

"And I shall get my courage," said the Lion, thoughtfully.

"And I shall get back to Kansas," cried Dorothy, clapping her hands. "Oh, let us start for the Emerald City to-morrow!"

This they decided to do. The next day they called the Winkies together and bade them good-bye. The Winkies were sorry to have them go, and they had grown so fond of the Tin Woodman that they begged him to stay and rule over them and the Yellow Land of the West. Finding they were determined to go, the Winkies gave Toto and the Lion each a golden collar; and to Dorothy they presented a beautiful bracelet, studded with diamonds; and to the Scarecrow they gave a gold-headed walking stick, to keep him from stumbling; and to the Tin Woodman they offered a silver oil-can, inlaid with gold and set with precious jewels.

Every one of the travellers made the Winkies a pretty speech in return, and all shook hands with them until their arms ached.

Dorothy went to the Witch's cupboard to fill her basket with food for the journey, and there she saw the Golden Cap. She tried it on her own head and found that it fitted her exactly. She did not know anything about the charm of the Golden Cap, but she saw that it was pretty, so she made up her mind to wear it and carry her sunbonnet in the basket.[31]

Then, being prepared for the journey, they all started for the Emerald City; and the Winkies gave them three cheers and many good wishes to carry with them.

# Chapter XIV.
# The Winged
# Monkeys

# You

will remember there was no road—not even a pathway—between the castle of the Wicked Witch and the Emerald City. When the four travellers went in search of the Witch she had seen them coming, and so sent the Winged Monkeys to bring them to her. It was much harder to find their way back through the big fields of buttercups and yellow daisies than it was being carried. They knew, of course, they must go straight east, toward the rising sun; and they started off in the right way. But at noon, when the sun was over their heads, they did not know which was east and which was west, and that was the reason they were lost in the great fields. They kept on walking, however, and at night the moon came out and shone brightly. So they lay down among the sweet smelling yellow flowers and slept soundly until morning—all but the Scarecrow and the Tin Woodman.

The next morning the sun was behind a cloud, but they started on, as if they were quite sure which way they were going.

"If we walk far enough," said Dorothy, "we shall sometime come to some place, I am sure."

But day by day passed away, and they still saw nothing before them but the yellow fields. The Scarecrow began to grumble a bit.

"We have surely lost our way," he said, "and unless we find it again in time to reach the Emerald City I shall never get my brains."

"Nor I my heart," declared the Tin Woodman, "It seems to me I can scarcely wait till I get to Oz, and you must admit this is a very long journey."

"You see," said the Cowardly Lion, with a whimper, "I haven't the courage to keep tramping forever, without getting anywhere at all."

Then Dorothy lost heart. She sat down on the grass and looked at her companions, and they sat down and looked at her, and Toto found that for the first time in his life he was too tired to chase a butterfly that flew past his head; so he put out his tongue and panted and looked at Dorothy as if to ask what they should do next.

"Suppose we call the field-mice," she suggested. "They could probably tell us the way to the Emerald City."

"To be sure they could," cried the Scarecrow; "why didn't we think of that before?"

Dorothy blew the little whistle she had always carried about her neck[32] since the Queen of the Mice had given it to her. In a few minutes they heard the pattering of tiny feet, and many of the small grey mice came running up to her. Among them was the Queen herself, who asked, in her squeaky little voice,

"What can I do for my friends?"

"We have lost our way," said Dorothy. "Can you tell us where the Emerald City is?"

"Certainly," answered the Queen; "but it is a great way off, for you have had it at your backs all this time." Then she noticed Dorothy's Golden Cap, and said, "Why don't you use the charm of the Cap, and call the Winged Monkeys to you? They will carry you to the City of Oz in less than an hour."

"I didn't know there was a charm," answered Dorothy in surprise. "What is it?"

"It is written inside the Golden Cap," replied the Queen of the Mice; "but if you are going to call the Winged Monkeys we must run away, for they are full of mischief and think it great fun to plague us."

"Won't they hurt me?" asked the girl, anxiously.

"Oh, no; they must obey the wearer of the Cap. Good-bye!" And she scampered out of sight, with all the mice hurrying after her.

Dorothy looked inside the Golden Cap and saw some words written upon the lining. These, she thought, must be the charm, so she read the directions carefully and put the Cap upon her head.

"Ep-pe, pep-pe, kak-ke!" she said, standing on her left foot.

"What did you say?" asked the Scarecrow, who did not know what she was doing.

"Hil-lo, hol-lo, hel-lo!" Dorothy went on, standing this time on her right foot.

"Hello!" replied the Tin Woodman, calmly.

"Ziz-zy, zuz-zy, zik!" said Dorothy, who was now standing on both feet. This ended the saying of the charm, and they heard a great chattering and flapping of wings, as the band of Winged Monkeys flew up to them. The King bowed low before Dorothy, and asked,

"What is your command?"

"We wish to go to the Emerald City," said the child, "and we have lost our way."

"We will carry you," replied the King, and no sooner had he spoken than two of the Monkeys caught Dorothy in their arms and flew away with her. Others took the Scarecrow and the Woodman and the Lion, and one little Monkey seized Toto and flew after them, although the dog tried hard to bite him.

The Scarecrow and the Tin Woodman were rather frightened at first, for they remembered how badly the Winged Monkeys had treated them before; but they saw that no harm was intended, so they rode through the air quite cheerfully, and had a fine time looking at the pretty gardens and woods far below them.

Dorothy found herself riding easily between two of the biggest Monkeys, one of them the King himself. They had made a chair of their hands and were careful not to hurt her.

"Why do you have to obey the charm of the Golden Cap?" she asked.

"That is a long story," answered the King, with a laugh; "but as we have a long journey before us I will pass the time by telling you about it, if you wish."

"I shall be glad to hear it," she replied.

*The Monkeys caught Dorothy in their arms and*
*flew away with her.*

"Once," began the leader, "we were a free people, living happily in the great forest, flying from tree to tree, eating nuts and fruit, and doing just as we pleased without calling anybody master. Perhaps some of us were rather too full of mischief at times, flying down to pull the tails of the animals that had no wings, chasing birds, and throwing nuts at the people who walked in the forest. But we were careless and happy and full of fun, and enjoyed every minute of the day. This was many years ago, long before Oz came out of the clouds to rule over this land.

"There lived here then, away at the North, a beautiful princess, who was also a powerful sorceress. All her magic was used to help the people, and she was never known to hurt anyone who was good. Her name was Gayelette, and she lived in a handsome palace built from great blocks of ruby. Everyone loved her, but her greatest sorrow was that she could find no one to love in return, since all the men were much too stupid and ugly to mate with one so beautiful and wise. At last, however, she found a boy who was handsome and manly and wise beyond his years. Gayelette made up her mind that when he grew to be a man she would make him her husband, so she took him to her ruby palace and used all her magic powers to make him as strong and good and lovely as any woman could wish. When he grew to manhood, Quelala, as he was called, was said to be the best and wisest man in all the land, while his manly beauty was so great that Gayelette loved him dearly, and hastened to make everything ready for the wedding.

"My grandfather was at that time the King of the Winged Monkeys which lived in the forest near Gayelette's palace, and the old fellow loved a joke better than a good dinner. One day, just before the wedding, my grandfather was flying out with his band when he saw Quelala walking beside the river. He was dressed in a rich costume of pink silk and purple velvet, and my grandfather thought he would see what he could do. At his word the band flew down and seized Quelala, carried him in their arms until they were over the middle of the river, and then dropped him into the water.

"'Swim out, my fine fellow,' cried my grandfather, 'and see if the water has spotted your clothes.' Quelala was much too wise not to swim, and he was not in the least spoiled by all his good fortune. He laughed, when he came to the top of the water, and swam in to shore. But when Gayelette came running out to him she found his silks and velvet all ruined by the river.

"The princess was very angry, and she knew, of course, who did it. She had all the Winged Monkeys brought before her, and she said at first that their wings should be tied and they should be treated as they had treated Quelala, and dropped in the river. But my grandfather pleaded hard, for he knew the Monkeys would drown in the river with their wings tied, and Quelala said a kind word for them also; so that Gayelette finally spared them, on condition that the Winged Monkeys should ever after do three times the bidding of the owner of the Golden Cap. This Cap had been made for a wedding present to Quelala, and it is said to have cost the princess half her kingdom. Of course my grandfather and all the other Monkeys at once agreed to the condition, and that is how it happens that we are three times the slaves of the owner of the Golden Cap, whomsoever he may be."

"And what became of them?" asked Dorothy, who had been greatly interested in the story.

"Quelala being the first owner of the Golden Cap," replied the Monkey, "he was the first to lay his wishes upon us. As his bride could not bear the sight of us, he called us all to him in the forest after he had married her and ordered us to always keep where she could never again set eyes on a Winged Monkey, which we were glad to do, for we were all afraid of her.

"This was all we ever had to do until the Golden Cap fell into the hands of the Wicked Witch of the West, who made us enslave the Winkies,[33] and afterward drive Oz himself out of the Land of the West. Now the Golden Cap is yours, and three times you have the right to lay your wishes upon us."

As the Monkey King finished his story Dorothy looked down and saw the green, shining walls of the Emerald City before them. She wondered at the rapid flight of the Monkeys, but was glad the journey was over. The strange creatures set the travellers down carefully before the gate of the City, the King bowed low to Dorothy, and then flew swiftly away, followed by all his band.

"That was a good ride," said the little girl.

"Yes, and a quick way out of our troubles," replied the Lion. "How lucky it was you brought away that wonderful Cap!"

# Chapter XV.
# The Discovery of
# OZ, The Terrible.

**T**he four travellers walked up to the great gate of the Emerald City and rang the bell. After ringing several times it was opened by the same Guardian of the Gates they had met before.

"What! are you back again?" he asked, in surprise.

"Do you not see us?" answered the Scarecrow.

"But I thought you had gone to visit the Wicked Witch of the West."

"We did visit her," said the Scarecrow.

"And she let you go again?" asked the man, in wonder.

"She could not help it, for she is melted," explained the Scarecrow.

"Melted! Well, that is good news, indeed," said the man. "Who melted her?"

"It was Dorothy," said the Lion, gravely.

"Good gracious!" exclaimed the man, and he bowed very low indeed before her.

Then he led them into his little room and locked the spectacles from the great box on all their eyes, just as he had done before. Afterward they passed on through the gate into the Emerald City, and when the people heard from the Guardian of the Gates that they had melted the Wicked Witch of the West they all gathered around the travellers and followed them in a great crowd to the Palace of Oz.

The soldier with the green whiskers was still on guard before the door, but he let them in at once and they were again met by the beautiful green girl, who showed each of them to their old rooms at once, so they might rest until the Great Oz was ready to receive them.

The soldier had the news carried straight to Oz that Dorothy and the other travellers had come back again, after destroying the Wicked Witch; but Oz made no reply. They thought the Great Wizard would send for them at once, but he did not. They had no word from him the next day, nor the next, nor the next. The waiting was tiresome and wearing, and at last they grew vexed that Oz should treat them in so poor a fashion, after sending them to undergo hardships and slavery. So the Scarecrow at last asked the green girl to take another message to Oz, saying if he did not let them in to see him at once they would call the Winged Monkeys to help them, and find out whether he kept his promises or not. When the Wizard was given this message he was so frightened that he sent word for them to come to the Throne Room at four minutes after nine o'clock the next morning.[34] He had once met the Winged Monkeys in the Land of the West,[35] and he did not wish to meet them again.

The four travellers passed a sleepless night, each thinking of the gift Oz had promised to bestow upon him. Dorothy fell asleep only once, and then she dreamed she was in Kansas, where Aunt Em was telling her how glad she was to have her little girl at home again.

Promptly at nine o'clock the next morning the green whiskered soldier came to them, and four minutes later they all went into the Throne Room of the Great Oz.

Of course each one of them expected to see the Wizard in the shape he had taken before, and all were greatly surprised when they looked about and saw no one at all in the room. They kept close to the door and closer to one another, for the stillness of the empty room was more dreadful than any of the forms they had seen Oz take.

Presently they heard a Voice, seeming to come from somewhere near the top of the great dome, and it said, solemnly:

"I am Oz, the Great and Terrible. Why do you seek me?"

They looked again in every part of the room, and then, seeing no one, Dorothy asked,

"Where are you?"

"I am everywhere,"[36] answered the Voice, "but to the eyes of common mortals I am invisible. I will now seat myself upon my throne, that you may converse with me." Indeed, the Voice seemed just then to come straight from the throne itself; so they walked toward it and stood in a row while Dorothy said:

"We have come to claim our promise, O Oz."

"What promise?" asked Oz.

"You promised to send me back to Kansas when the Wicked Witch was destroyed," said the girl.

"And you promised to give me brains," said the Scarecrow.

"And you promised to give me a heart," said the Tin Woodman.

"And you promised to give me courage," said the Cowardly Lion.

"Is the Wicked Witch really destroyed?" asked the Voice, and Dorothy thought it trembled a little.

"Yes," she answered, "I melted her with a bucket of water."

"Dear me," said the Voice; "how sudden! Well, come to me to-morrow, for I must have time to think it over."

"You've had plenty of time already," said the Tin Woodman, angrily.

"We shan't wait a day longer," said the Scarecrow.

"You must keep your promises to us!" exclaimed Dorothy.

The Lion thought it might be as well to frighten the Wizard, so he gave a large, loud roar, which was so fierce and dreadful that Toto jumped away from him in alarm and tipped over the screen that stood in a corner. As it fell with a crash they looked that way, and the next moment all of them were filled with wonder. For they saw, standing in just the spot the screen had hidden, a little, old man, with a bald head and a wrinkled face, who seemed to be as much surprised as they were. The Tin Woodman, raising his axe, rushed toward the little man and cried out,

"Who are you?"

"I am Oz, the Great and Terrible," said the little man,[37] in a trembling voice, "but don't strike me—please don't!—and I'll do anything you want me to."

Our friends looked at him in surprise and dismay.

"I thought Oz was a great Head," said Dorothy.

"And I thought Oz was a lovely Lady," said the Scarecrow.

"And I thought Oz was a terrible Beast," said the Tin Woodman.

"And I thought Oz was a Ball of Fire," exclaimed the Lion.

"No; you are all wrong," said the little man, meekly. "I have been making believe."

"Making believe!" cried Dorothy. "Are you not a great Wizard?"

"Hush, my dear," he said; "don't speak so loud, or you will be overheard—and I should be ruined. I'm supposed to be a Great Wizard."

"And aren't you?" she asked.

"Not a bit of it, my dear; I'm just a common man."

"You're more than that," said the Scarecrow, in a grieved tone; "you're a humbug."*

"Exactly so!" declared the little man, rubbing his hands together as if it pleased him; "I am a humbug."

"But this is terrible," said the Tin Woodman; "how shall I ever get my heart?"

"Or I my courage?" asked the Lion.

"Or I my brains?" wailed the Scarecrow, wiping the the tears from his eyes with his coat-sleeve.

"My dear friends," said Oz, "I pray you not to speak of these little things. Think of me, and the terrible trouble I'm in at being found out."

"Doesn't anyone else know you're a humbug?" asked Dorothy.

"No one knows it but you four—and myself," replied Oz. "I have fooled everyone so long that I thought I should never be found out. It was a great mistake my ever letting you into the Throne Room.

---

*A fraud.

*"Exactly so! I am a humbug."*

Usually I will not see even my subjects, and so they believe I am something terrible."

"But, I don't understand," said Dorothy, in bewilderment. "How was it that you appeared to me as a great Head?"

"That was one of my tricks," answered Oz. "Step this way, please, and I will tell you all about it."

He led the way to a small chamber in the rear of the Throne Room, and they all followed him. He pointed to one corner, in which lay the Great Head, made out of many thicknesses of paper, and with a carefully painted face.

"This I hung from the ceiling by a wire," said Oz; "I stood behind the screen and pulled a thread, to make the eyes move and the mouth open."

"But how about the voice?" she enquired.

"Oh, I am a ventriloquist," said the little man, "and I can throw the sound of my voice wherever I wish; so that you thought it was coming out of the Head. Here are the other things I used to deceive you." He showed the Scarecrow the dress and the mask he had worn when he seemed to be the lovely Lady; and the Tin Woodman saw that his Terrible Beast was nothing but a lot of skins, sewn together, with slats to keep their sides out. As for the Ball of Fire, the false Wizard had hung that also from the ceiling. It was really a ball of cotton, but when oil was poured upon it the ball burned fiercely.

"Really," said the Scarecrow, "you ought to be ashamed of yourself for being such a humbug."

"I am—I certainly am," answered the little man, sorrowfully; "but it was the only thing I could do. Sit down, please, there are plenty of chairs; and I will tell you my story."

So they sat down and listened while he told the following tale:

"I was born in Omaha—"

"Why, that isn't very far from Kansas!" cried Dorothy.

"No; but it's farther from here," he said, shaking his head at her, sadly. "When I grew up I became a ventriloquist, and at that I was very well trained by a great master. I can imitate any kind of a bird or beast." Here he mewed so like a kitten that Toto pricked up his ears and looked everywhere to see where she was. "After a time," continued Oz, "I tired of that, and became a balloonist."

"What is that?" asked Dorothy.

"A man who goes up in a balloon on circus day, so as to draw a crowd of people together and get them to pay to see the circus," he explained.

"Oh," she said; "I know."

"Well, one day I went up in a balloon and the ropes got twisted, so that I couldn't come down again. It went way up above the clouds, so far that a current of air struck it and carried it many, many miles away. For a day and a night I travelled through the air, and on the morning of the second day I awoke and found the balloon floating over a strange and beautiful country.[38]

"It came down gradually, and I was not hurt a bit. But I found myself in the midst of a strange people, who, seeing me come from the clouds, thought I was a great Wizard. Of course I let them think so, because they were afraid of me, and promised to do anything I wished them to.

"Just to amuse myself, and keep the good people busy, I ordered them to build this City, and my Palace; and they did it all willingly and well. Then I thought, as the country was so green and beautiful, I would call it the Emerald City, and to make the name fit better I put green spectacles on all the people, so that everything they saw was green."

"But isn't everything here green?" asked Dorothy.

"No more than in any other city," replied Oz; "but when you wear green spectacles, why of course everything you see looks green to you. The Emerald City was built a great many years ago, for I was a young man when the balloon brought me here, and I am a very old man now. But my people have worn green glasses on their eyes so long that most of them think it really is an Emerald City, and it certainly is a beautiful place, abounding in jewels and precious metals, and every good thing that is needed to make one happy. I have been good to the people, and they like me; but ever since this Palace was built I have shut myself up and would not see any of them.

"One of my greatest fears was the Witches, for while I had no magical powers at all I soon found out that the Witches were really able to do wonderful things. There were four of them in this country, and they ruled the people who live in the North and South and

East and West. Fortunately, the Witches of the North and South were good, and I knew they would do me no harm; but the Witches of the East and West were terribly wicked, and had they not thought I was more powerful than they themselves, they would surely have destroyed me. As it was, I lived in deadly fear of them for many years; so you can imagine how pleased I was when I heard your house had fallen on the Wicked Witch of the East. When you came to me I was willing to promise anything if you would only do away with the other Witch; but, now that you have melted her, I am ashamed to say that I cannot keep my promises."

"I think you are a very bad man," said Dorothy.

"Oh, no, my dear; I'm really a very good man; but I'm a very bad Wizard, I must admit."

"Can't you give me brains?" asked the Scarecrow.

"You don't need them. You are learning something every day. A baby has brains, but it doesn't know much. Experience is the only thing that brings knowledge, and the longer you are on earth the more experience you are sure to get."

"That may all be true," said the Scarecrow, "but I shall be very unhappy unless you give me brains."

The false Wizard looked at him carefully.

"Well," he said, with a sigh, "I'm not much of a magician, as I said; but if you will come to me to-morrow morning, I will stuff your head with brains. I cannot tell you how to use them, however; you must find that out for yourself."

"Oh, thank you—thank you!" cried the Scarecrow. "I'll find a way to use them, never fear!"

"But how about my courage?" asked the Lion, anxiously.

"You have plenty of courage, I am sure," answered Oz. "All you need is confidence in yourself. There is no living thing that is not afraid when it faces danger. True courage is in facing danger when you are afraid, and that kind of courage you have in plenty."

"Perhaps I have, but I'm scared just the same," said the Lion. "I shall really be very unhappy unless you give me the sort of courage that makes one forget he is afraid."

"Very well; I will give you that sort of courage to-morrow," replied Oz.

"How about my heart?" asked the Tin Woodman.

"Why, as for that," answered Oz, "I think you are wrong to want a heart. It makes most people unhappy. If you only knew it, you are in luck not to have a heart."

"That must be a matter of opinion," said the Tin Woodman. "For my part, I will bear all the unhappiness without a murmur, if you will give me the heart."

"Very well," answered Oz, meekly. "Come to me to-morrow and you shall have a heart. I have played Wizard for so many years that I may as well continue the part a little longer."

"And now," said Dorothy, "how am I to get back to Kansas?"

"We shall have to think about that," replied the little man, "Give me two or three days to consider the matter and I'll try to find a way to carry you over the desert. In the meantime you shall all be treated as my guests, and while you live in the Palace my people will wait upon you and obey your slighest wish. There is only one thing I ask in return for my help—such as it is. You must keep my secret and tell no one I am a humbug."

They agreed to say nothing of what they had learned, and went back to their rooms in high spirits. Even Dorothy had hope that "The Great and Terrible Humbug," as she called him, would find a way to send her back to Kansas, and if he did that she was willing to forgive him everything.

# Chapter XVI.
## The Magic Art of the Great Humbug.

# Next

morning the Scarecrow said to his friends:

"Congratulate me. I am going to Oz to get my brains at last. When I return I shall be as other men are."

"I have always liked you as you were," said Dorothy, simply.

"It is kind of you to like a Scarecrow," he replied. "But surely you will think more of me when you hear the splendid thoughts my new brain is going to turn out." Then he said good-bye to them all in a cheerful voice and went to the Throne Room, where he rapped upon the door.

"Come in," said Oz.

The Scarecrow went in and found the little man sitting down by the window, engaged in deep thought.

"I have come for my brains," remarked the Scarecrow, a little uneasily.

"Oh, yes; sit down in that chair, please," replied Oz. "You must excuse me for taking your head off, but I shall have to do it in order to put your brains in their proper place."

"That's all right," said the Scarecrow. "You are quite welcome to take my head off, as long as it will be a better one when you put it on again."

So the Wizard unfastened his head and emptied out the straw. Then he entered the back room and took up a measure of bran,* which he mixed with a great many pins and needles. Having shaken them together thoroughly, he filled the top of the Scarecrow's head with the mixture and stuffed the rest of the space with straw, to hold it in place. When he had fastened the Scarecrow's head on his body again he said to him,

"Hereafter you will be a great man, for I have given you a lot of bran-new brains."[39]

The Scarecrow was both pleased and proud at the fulfillment of his greatest wish, and having thanked Oz warmly he went back to his friends.

Dorothy looked at him curiously. His head was quite bulging out at the top with brains.

"How do you feel?" she asked.

"I feel wise, indeed," he answered, earnestly. "When I get used to my brains I shall know everything."

"Why are those needles and pins sticking out of your head?" asked the Tin Woodman.

"That is proof that he is sharp," remarked the Lion.

"Well, I must go to Oz and get my heart," said the Woodman. So he walked to the Throne Room and knocked at the door.

"Come in," called Oz, and the Woodman entered and said,

"I have come for my heart."

"Very well," answered the little man. "But I shall have to cut a hole in your breast, so I can put your heart in the right place. I hope it won't hurt you."

"Oh, no;" answered the Woodman. "I shall not feel it at all."

So Oz brought a pair of tinners' shears and cut a small, square hole in the left side of the Tin Woodman's breast. Then, going to a chest of drawers, he took out a pretty heart, made entirely of silk and stuffed with sawdust.

---

*A cereal grain.

*"I feel wise, indeed,"* said the Scarecrow.

"Isn't it a beauty?" he asked.

"It is, indeed!" replied the Woodman, who was greatly pleased. "But is it a kind heart?"

"Oh, very!" answered Oz. He put the heart in the Woodman's breast and then replaced the square of tin, soldering it neatly together where it had been cut.

"There," said he; "now you have a heart that any man might be proud of. I'm sorry I had to put a patch on your breast, but it really couldn't be helped."

"Never mind the patch," exclaimed the happy Woodman. "I am very grateful to you, and shall never forget your kindness."

"Don't speak of it," replied Oz.

Then the Tin Woodman went back to his friends, who wished him every joy on account of his good fortune.

The Lion now walked to the Throne Room and knocked at the door.

"Come in," said Oz.

"I have come for my courage," announced the Lion, entering the room.

"Very well," answered the little man; "I will get it for you."

He went to a cupboard and reaching up to a high shelf took down a square green bottle, the contents of which he poured into a green-gold dish, beautifully carved. Placing this before the Cowardly Lion, who sniffed at it as if he did not like it, the Wizard said,

"Drink."

"What is it?" asked the Lion.

"Well," answered Oz, "if it were inside of you, it would be courage. You know, of course, that courage is always inside one; so that this really cannot be called courage until you have swallowed it. Therefore I advise you to drink it as soon as possible."

The Lion hesitated no longer, but drank till the dish was empty.

"How do you feel now?" asked Oz.

"Full of courage," replied the Lion, who went joyfully back to his friends to tell them of his good fortune.

Oz, left to himself, smiled to think of his success in giving the Scarecrow and the Tin Woodman and the Lion exactly what they thought they wanted. "How can I help being a humbug," he said, "when all these people make me do things that everybody knows can't be done? It was easy to make the Scarecrow and the Lion and the Woodman happy, because they imagined I could do anything. But it will take more than imagination to carry Dorothy back to Kansas, and I'm sure I don't know how it can be done."

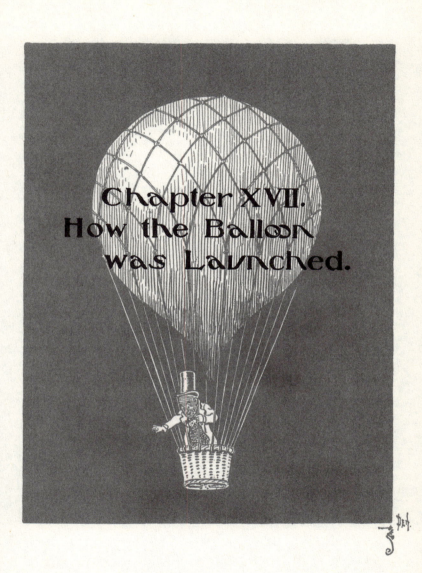

Chapter XVII.
How the Balloon
was Launched.

**F**or three days Dorothy heard nothing from Oz. These were sad days for the little girl, although her friends were all quite happy and contented. The Scarecrow told them there were wonderful thoughts in his head; but he would not say what they were because he knew no one could understand them but himself. When the Tin Woodman walked about he felt his heart rattling around in his breast; and he told Dorothy he had discovered it to be a kinder and more tender heart than the one he had owned when he was made of flesh. The Lion declared he was afraid of nothing on earth, and would gladly face an army of men or a dozen of the fierce Kalidahs.

Thus each of the little party was satisfied except Dorothy, who longed more than ever to get back to Kansas.

On the fourth day, to her great joy, Oz sent for her, and when she entered the Throne Room he said, pleasantly:

"Sit down, my dear; I think I have found the way to get you out of this country."

"And back to Kansas?" she asked, eagerly.

"Well, I'm not sure about Kansas," said Oz; "for I haven't the faintest notion which way it lies. But the first thing to do is to cross the desert, and then it should be easy to find your way home."

"How can I cross the desert?" she enquired.

"Well, I'll tell you what I think," said the little man. "You see, when I came to this country it was in a balloon. You also came through the air, being carried by a cyclone. So I believe the best way to get across the desert will be through the air. Now, it is quite beyond my powers to make a cyclone; but I've been thinking the matter over, and I believe I can make a balloon."

"How?" asked Dorothy.

"A balloon," said Oz, "is made of silk, which is coated with glue to keep the gas in it. I have plenty of silk in the Palace, so it will be no trouble for us to make the balloon. But in all this country there is no gas to fill the balloon with, to make it float."

"If it won't float," remarked Dorothy, "it will be of no use to us."

"True," answered Oz. "But there is another way to make it float, which is to fill it with hot air. Hot air isn't as good as gas,[40] for if the air should get cold the balloon would come down in the desert, and we should be lost."

"We!" exclaimed the girl; "are you going with me?"

"Yes, of course," replied Oz. "I am tired of being such a humbug. If I should go out of this Palace my people would soon discover I am not a Wizard, and then they would be vexed with me for having deceived them. So I have to stay shut up in these rooms all day, and it gets tiresome. I'd much rather go back to Kansas with you and be in a circus again."

"I shall be glad to have your company," said Dorothy.

"Thank you," he answered. "Now, if you will help me sew the silk together, we will begin to work on our balloon."

So Dorothy took a needle and thread, and as fast as Oz cut the strips of silk into proper shape the girl sewed them neatly together. First there was a strip of light green silk, then a strip of dark green and then a strip of emerald green; for Oz had a fancy to make the balloon in different shades of the color about them. It took three days to sew all the strips together, but when it was finished they had a big bag of green silk more than twenty feet long.

Then Oz painted it on the inside with a coat of thin glue, to make it air-tight, after which he announced that the balloon was ready.

"But we must have a basket to ride in," he said. So he sent the soldier with the green whiskers for a big clothes basket, which he fastened with many ropes to the bottom of the balloon.

When it was all ready, Oz sent word to his people that he was going to make a visit to a great brother Wizard who lived in the clouds. The news spread rapidly throughout the city and everyone came to see the wonderful sight.

Oz ordered the balloon carried out in front of the Palace, and the people gazed upon it with much curiosity. The Tin Woodman had chopped a big pile of wood, and now he made a fire of it, and Oz held the bottom of the balloon over the fire so that the hot air that arose from it would be caught in the silken bag. Gradually the balloon swelled out and rose into the air, until finally the basket just touched the ground.

Then Oz got into the basket and said to all the people in a loud voice:

"I am now going away to make a visit. While I am gone the Scarecrow will rule over you. I command you to obey him as you would me."

The balloon was by this time tugging hard at the rope that held it to the ground, for the air within it was hot, and this made it so much lighter in weight than the air without that it pulled hard to rise into the sky.

"Come, Dorothy!" cried the Wizard; "hurry up, or the balloon will fly away."

"I can't find Toto anywhere," replied Dorothy, who did not wish to leave her little dog behind. Toto had run into the crowd to bark at a kitten, and Dorothy at last found him. She picked him up and ran toward the balloon.

She was within a few steps of it, and Oz was holding out his hands to help her into the basket, when, crack! went the ropes, and the balloon rose into the air without her.

"Come back!" she screamed; "I want to go, too!"

"I can't come back, my dear," called Oz from the basket. "Good-bye!"

"Good-bye!" shouted everyone, and all eyes were turned upward to where the Wizard was riding in the basket, rising every moment farther and farther into the sky.

And that was the last any of them ever saw of Oz, the Wonderful Wizard, though he may have reached Omaha safely, and be there now, for all we know. But the people remembered him lovingly, and said to one another,

"Oz was always our friend. When he was here he built for us this beautiful Emerald City, and now he is gone he has left the Wise Scarecrow to rule over us,"

Still, for many days they grieved over the loss of the Wonderful Wizard, and would not be comforted.

# Chapter XVIII.
## Away to the South.

**D**orothy wept bitterly at the passing of her hope to get home to Kansas again; but when she thought it all over she was glad she had not gone up in a balloon. And she also felt sorry at losing Oz, and so did her companions.

The Tin Woodman came to her and said,

"Truly I should be ungrateful if I failed to mourn for the man who gave me my lovely heart. I should like to cry a little because Oz is gone, if you will kindly wipe away my tears, so that I shall not rust."

"With pleasure," she answered, and brought a towel at once. Then the Tin Woodman wept for several minutes, and she watched the tears carefully and wiped them away with the towel. When he had finished he thanked her kindly and oiled himself thoroughly with his jewelled oil-can, to guard against mishap.

The Scarecrow was now the ruler of the Emerald City, and although he was not a Wizard the people were proud of him. "For," they said, "there is not another city in all the world that is ruled by a stuffed man." And, so far as they knew, they were quite right.

The morning after the balloon had gone up with Oz the four travellers met in the Throne Room and talked matters over. The Scarecrow sat in the big throne and the others stood respectfully before him.

"We are not so unlucky," said the new ruler; "for this Palace and the Emerald City belong to us, and we can do just as we please. When I remember that a short time ago I was up on a pole in a farmer's cornfield, and that I am now the ruler of this beautiful City, I am quite satisfied with my lot."

"I also," said the Tin Woodman, "am well pleased with my new heart; and, really, that was the only thing I wished in all the world."

"For my part, I am content in knowing I am as brave as any beast that ever lived, if not braver," said the Lion, modestly.

"If Dorothy would only be contented to live in the Emerald City," continued the Scarecrow, "we might all be happy together."

"But I don't want to live here," cried Dorothy. "I want to go to Kansas, and live with Aunt Em and Uncle Henry."

"Well, then, what can be done?" enquired the Woodman.

The Scarecrow decided to think, and he thought so hard that the pins and needles began to stick out of his brains. Finally he said:

"Why not call the Winged Monkeys, and asked them to carry you over the desert?"

"I never thought of that!" said Dorothy, joyfully. "It's just the thing. I'll go at once for the Golden Cap."

When she brought it into the Throne Room she spoke the magic words, and soon the band of Winged Monkeys flew in through an open window and stood beside her.

"This is the second time you have called us," said the Monkey King, bowing before the little girl. "What do you wish?"

"I want you to fly with me to Kansas," said Dorothy.

But the Monkey King shook his head.

"That cannot be done," he said. "We belong to this country alone, and cannot leave it. There has never been a Winged Monkey in Kansas yet, and I suppose there never will be, for they don't belong there. We shall be glad to serve you in any way in our power, but we cannot cross the desert. Good-bye."

And with another bow the Monkey King spread his wings and flew away through the window, followed by all his band.

*The Scarecrow sat on the big throne.*

Dorothy was almost ready to cry with disappointment.

"I have wasted the charm of the Golden Cap to no purpose," she said, "for the Winged Monkeys cannot help me."

"It is certainly too bad!" said the tender hearted Woodman.

The Scarecrow was thinking again, and his head bulged out so horribly that Dorothy feared it would burst.

"Let us call in the soldier with the green whiskers," he said, "and ask his advice."

So the soldier was summoned and entered the Throne Room timidly, for while Oz was alive he never was allowed to come further than the door.

"This little girl," said the Scarecrow to the soldier, "wishes to cross the desert. How can she do so?"

"I cannot tell," answered the soldier; "for nobody has ever crossed the desert, unless it is Oz himself."

"Is there no one who can help me?" asked Dorothy, earnestly.

"Glinda might," he suggested.

"Who is Glinda?" enquired the Scarecrow.

"The Witch of the South. She is the most powerful of all the Witches, and rules over the Quadlings. Besides, her castle stands on the edge of the desert, so she may know a way to cross it."

"Glinda is a good Witch, isn't she?" asked the child.

"The Quadlings think she is good," said the soldier, "and she is kind to everyone. I have heard that Glinda is a beautiful woman,[41] who knows how to keep young in spite of the many years she has lived."

"How can I get to her castle?" asked Dorothy.

"The road is straight to the South," he answered, "but it is said to be full of dangers to travellers. There are wild beasts in the woods, and a race of queer men who do not like strangers to cross their country. For this reason none of the Quadlings ever come to the Emerald City."

The soldier then left them and the Scarecrow said,

"It seems, in spite of dangers, that the best thing Dorothy can do is to travel to the Land of the South and ask Glinda to help her. For, of course, if Dorothy stays here she will never get back to Kansas."

"You must have been thinking again," remarked the Tin Woodman.

"I have," said the Scarecrow.

"I shall go with Dorothy," declared the Lion, "for I am tired of your city and long for the woods and the country again. I am really a wild beast, you know. Besides, Dorothy will need someone to protect her."

"That is true," agreed the Woodman. "My axe may be of service to her; so I, also, will go with her to the Land of the South."

"When shall we start?" asked the Scarecrow.

"Are you going?" they asked, in surprise.

"Certainly. If it wasn't for Dorothy I should never have had brains. She lifted me from the pole in the cornfield and brought me to the Emerald City. So my good luck is all due to her, and I shall never leave her until she starts back to Kansas for good and all."

"Thank you," said Dorothy, gratefully. "You are all very kind to me. But I should like to start as soon as possible."

"We shall go to-morrow morning," returned the Scarecrow. "So now let us all get ready, for it will be a long journey."

Chapter XIX.
Attacked by the
Fighting Trees.

# The

next morning Dorothy kissed the pretty green girl good-bye, and they all shook hands with the soldier with the green whiskers, who had walked with them as far as the gate. When the Guardian of the Gates saw them again he wondered greatly that they could leave the beautiful City to get into new trouble. But he at once unlocked their spectacles, which he put back into the green box, and gave them many good wishes to carry with them.

"You are now our ruler," he said to the Scarecrow; "so you must come back to us as soon as possible."

"I certainly shall if I am able," the Scarecrow replied; "but I must help Dorothy to get home, first."

As Dorothy bade the good-natured Guardian a last farewell she said,

"I have been very kindly treated in your lovely City, and everyone has been good to me. I cannot tell you how grateful I am."

"Don't try, my dear," he answered. "We should like to keep you with us, but if it is your wish to return to Kansas I hope you will find a way." He then opened the gate of the outer wall and they walked forth and started upon their journey.

The sun shone brightly as our friends turned their faces toward the Land of the South. They were all in the best of spirits, and laughed and chatted together. Dorothy was once more filled with the hope of getting home, and the Scarecrow and the Tin Woodman were glad to be of use to her. As for the Lion, he sniffed the fresh air with delight and whisked his tail from side to side in pure joy at being in the country again, while Toto ran around them and chased the moths and butterflies, barking merrily all the time.

"City life does not agree with me at all," remarked the Lion, as they walked along at a brisk pace. "I have lost much flesh since I lived there, and now I am anxious for a chance to show the other beasts how courageous I have grown."

They now turned and took a last look at the Emerald City. All they could see was a mass of towers and steeples behind the green walls, and high up above everything the spires and dome of the Palace of Oz.

"Oz was not such a bad Wizard, after all," said the Tin Woodman, as he felt his heart rattling around in his breast.

"He knew how to give me brains, and very good brains, too," said the Scarecrow.

"If Oz had taken a dose of the same courage he gave me," added the Lion, "he would have been a brave man."

Dorothy said nothing. Oz had not kept the promise he made her, but he had done his best, so she forgave him. As he said, he was a good man, even if he was a bad Wizard.

The first day's journey was through the green fields and bright flowers that stretched about the Emerald City on every side. They slept that night on the grass, with nothing but the stars over them; and they rested very well indeed.

In the morning they travelled on until they came to a thick wood. There was no way of going around it, for it seemed to extend to the right and left as far as they could see; and, besides, they did not dare change the direction of their journey for fear of getting lost. So they looked for the place where it would be easiest to get into the forest.

The Scarecrow, who was in the lead, finally discovered a big tree with such wide spreading branches that there was room for the party to pass underneath. So he walked forward to the tree, but just as he came under the first branches they bent down and twined around him, and the next minute he was raised from the ground and flung headlong among his fellow travellers.

This did not hurt the Scarecrow, but it surprised him, and he looked rather dizzy when Dorothy picked him up.

"Here is another space between the trees," called the Lion.

"Let me try it first," said the Scarecrow, "for it doesn't hurt me to get thrown about." He walked up to another tree, as he spoke, but its branches immediately seized him and tossed him back again.

"This is strange," exclaimed Dorothy; "what shall we do?"

"The trees seem to have made up their minds to fight us, and stop our journey," remarked the Lion.

"I believe I will try it myself," said the Woodman, and shouldering his axe he marched up to the first tree that had handled the Scarecrow so roughly. When a big branch bent down to seize him the Woodman chopped at it so fiercely that he cut it in two. At once the tree began shaking all its branches as if in pain, and the Tin Woodman passed safely under it.

"Come on!" he shouted to the others; "be quick!"

They all ran forward and passed under the tree without injury, except Toto, who was caught by a small branch and shaken until he howled. But the Woodman promptly chopped off the branch and set the little dog free.

The other trees of the forest did nothing to keep them back, so they made up their minds that only the first row of trees could bend down their branches, and that probably these were the policemen of the forest, and given this wonderful power in order to keep strangers out of it.

The four travellers walked with ease through the trees until they came to the further edge of the wood. Then, to their surprise, they found before them a high wall, which seemed to be made of white china. It was smooth, like the surface of a dish, and higher than their heads.

"What shall we do now?" asked Dorothy.

"I will make a ladder," said the Tin Woodman, "for we certainly must climb over the wall."

*The branches bent down and twined around him.*

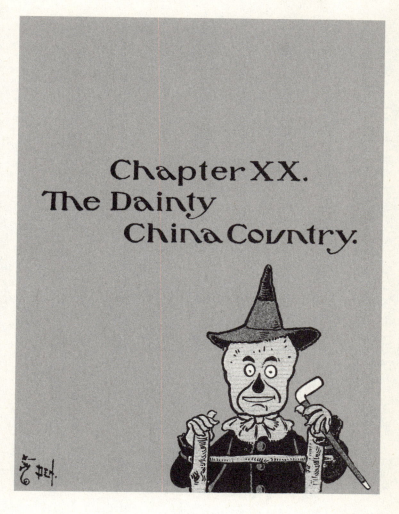

# Chapter XX.
## The Dainty
### China Country.

the Woodman was
making a ladder from
wood which he found in the forest Dorothy lay down and slept, for she
was tired by the long walk. The Lion also
curled himself up to sleep and Toto lay beside him.

The Scarecrow watched the Woodman while he worked, and
said to him:

"I cannot think why this wall is here, nor what it is made of."

"Rest your brains and do not worry about the wall," replied the
Woodman; "when we have climbed over it we shall know what is
on the other side."

After a time the ladder was finished. It looked clumsy, but the
Tin Woodman was sure it was strong and would answer their purpose. The Scarecrow waked Dorothy and the Lion and Toto, and
told them that the ladder was ready. The Scarecrow climbed up the
ladder first, but he was so awkward that Dorothy had to follow close
behind and keep him from falling off. When he got his head over
the top of the wall the Scarecrow said,

"Oh, my!"

"Go on," exclaimed Dorothy.

So the Scarecrow climbed further up and sat down on the top of the wall, and Dorothy put her head over and cried,

"Oh, my!" just as the Scarecrow had done.

Then Toto came up, and immediately began to bark, but Dorothy made him be still.

The Lion climbed the ladder next, and the Tin Woodman came last; but both of them cried, "Oh, my!" as soon as they looked over the wall. When they were all sitting in a row on the top of the wall they looked down and saw a strange sight.

Before them was a great stretch of country having a floor as smooth and shining and white as the bottom of a big platter. Scattered around were many houses made entirely of china and painted in the brightest colors. These houses were quite small, the biggest of them reaching only as high as Dorothy's waist. There were also pretty little barns, with china fences around them, and many cows and sheep and horses and pigs and chickens, all made of china, were standing about in groups.

But the strangest of all were the people who lived in this queer country. There were milk-maids and shepherdesses, with bright-colored bodices* and golden spots all over their gowns; and princesses with most gorgeous frocks of silver and gold and purple; and shepherds dressed in knee-breeches with pink and yellow and blue stripes down them, and golden buckles on their shoes; and princes with jewelled crowns upon their heads, wearing ermine† robes and satin doublets; and funny clowns in ruffled gowns, with round red spots upon their cheeks and tall, pointed caps. And, strangest of all, these people were all made of china, even to their clothes, and were so small that the tallest of them was no higher than Dorothy's knee.

No one did so much as look at the travellers at first, except one little purple china dog with an extra-large head, which came to the wall and barked at them in a tiny voice, afterwards running away again.

"How shall we get down?" asked Dorothy.

---

*Upper portion of a dress or gown.
†Expensive white fur used to line or trim ceremonial robes.

*These people were all made of china.*

They found the ladder so heavy they could not pull it up, so the Scarecrow fell off the wall and the others jumped down upon him so that the hard floor would not hurt their feet. Of course they took pains not to light on his head and get the pins in their feet. When all were safely down they picked up the Scarecrow, whose body was quite flattened out, and patted his straw into shape again.

"We must cross this strange place in order to get to the other side," said Dorothy; "for it would be unwise for us to go any other way except due South."

They began walking through the country of the china people, and the first thing they came to was a china milk-maid milking a china cow. As they drew near the cow suddenly gave a kick and kicked over the stool, the pail, and even the milk-maid herself, all falling on the china ground with a great clatter.

Dorothy was shocked to see that the cow had broken her leg short off, and that the pail was lying in several small pieces, while the poor milk-maid had a nick in her left elbow.

"There!" cried the milk-maid, angrily; "see what you have done! My cow has broken her leg, and I must take her to the mender's shop and have it glued on again. What do you mean by coming here and frightening my cow?"

"I'm very sorry," returned Dorothy; "please forgive us."

But the pretty milk-maid was much too vexed to make any answer. She picked up the leg sulkily and led her cow away, the poor animal limping on three legs. As she left them the milk-maid cast many reproachful glances over her shoulder at the clumsy strangers, holding her nicked elbow close to her side.

Dorothy was quite grieved at this mishap.

"We must be very careful here," said the kind-hearted Woodman, "or we may hurt these pretty little people so they will never get over it."

A little farther on Dorothy met a most beautifully dressed young princess, who stopped short as she saw the strangers and started to run away.

Dorothy wanted to see more of the Princess, so she ran after her; but the china girl cried out,

"Don't chase me! don't chase me!"

She had such a frightened little voice that Dorothy stopped and said,

"Why not?"

"Because," answered the Princess, also stopping, a safe distance away, "if I run I may fall down and break myself."

"But couldn't you be mended?" asked the girl.

"Oh, yes; but one is never so pretty after being mended, you know," replied the Princess.

"I suppose not," said Dorothy.

"Now there is Mr. Joker, one of our clowns," continued the china lady, "who is always trying to stand upon his head. He has broken himself so often that he is mended in a hundred places, and doesn't look at all pretty. Here he comes now, so you can see for yourself."

Indeed, a jolly little Clown now came walking toward them, and Dorothy could see that in spite of his pretty clothes of red and yellow and green he was completely covered with cracks, running every which way and showing plainly that he had been mended in many places.

The Clown put his hands in his pockets, and after puffing out his cheeks and nodding his head at them saucily he said,

> *"My lady fair,*
> *Why do you stare*
> *At poor old Mr. Joker?*
> *You're quite as stiff*
> *And prim as if*
> *You'd eaten up a poker!"**

"Be quiet, sir!" said the Princess; "can't you see these are strangers, and should be treated with respect?"

"Well, that's respect, I expect," declared the Clown, and immediately stood upon his head.

"Don't mind Mr. Joker," said the Princess to Dorothy; "he is considerably cracked in his head, and that makes him foolish."

---

*Metal rod or bar used to tend a fire.

"Oh, I don't mind him a bit," said Dorothy. "But you are so beautiful," she continued, "that I am sure I could love you dearly. Won't you let me carry you back to Kansas and stand you on Aunt Em's mantle-shelf? I could carry you in my basket."

"That would make me very unhappy," answered the China Princess. "You see, here in our own country we live contentedly, and can talk and move around as we please. But whenever any of us are taken away our joints at once stiffen, and we can only stand straight and look pretty. Of course that is all that is expected of us when we are on mantle-shelves and cabinets and drawing-room tables, but our lives are much pleasanter here in our own country."

"I would not make you unhappy for all the world!" exclaimed Dorothy; "so I'll just say good-bye."

"Good-bye," replied the Princess.

They walked carefully through the china country. The little animals and all the people scampered out of their way, fearing the strangers would break them, and after an hour or so the travellers reached the other side of the country and came to another china wall.

It was not as high as the first, however, and by standing upon the Lion's back they all managed to scramble to the top. Then the Lion gathered his legs under him and jumped on the wall; but just as he jumped he upset a china church with his tail and smashed it all to pieces.[43]

"That was too bad," said Dorothy, "but really I think we were lucky in not doing these little people more harm than breaking a cow's leg and a church. They are all so brittle!"

"They are, indeed," said the Scarecrow, "and I am thankful I am made of straw and cannot be easily damaged. There are worse things in the world than being a Scarecrow."

# Chapter XXI.
# The Lion Becomes
# the King of Beasts.

**A**fter climbing down from the china wall the travellers found themselves in a disagreeable country, full of bogs and marshes and covered with tall, rank grass. It was difficult to walk far without falling into muddy holes, for the grass was so thick that it hid them from sight. However, by carefully picking their way, they got safely along until they reached solid ground. But here the country seemed wilder than ever, and after a long and tiresome walk through the underbrush they entered another forest, where the trees were bigger and older than any they had ever seen.

"This forest is perfectly delightful," declared the Lion, looking around him with joy; "never have I seen a more beautiful place."

"It seems gloomy," said the Scarecrow.

"Not a bit of it," answered the Lion; "I should like to live here all my life. See how soft the dried leaves are under your feet and how rich and green the moss is that clings to these old trees. Surely no wild beast could wish a pleasanter home."

"Perhaps there are wild beasts in the forest now," said Dorothy.

"I suppose there are," returned the Lion; "but I do not see any of them about."

They walked through the forest until it became too dark to go any farther. Dorothy and Toto and the Lion lay down to sleep, while the Woodman and the Scarecrow kept watch over them as usual.

When morning came they started again. Before they had gone far they heard a low rumble, as of the growling of many wild animals. Toto whimpered a little but none of the others was frightened and they kept along the well-trodden path until they came to an opening in the wood, in which were gathered hundreds of beasts of every variety. There were tigers and elephants and bears and wolves and foxes and all the others in the natural history, and for a moment Dorothy was afraid. But the Lion explained that the animals were holding a meeting, and he judged by their snarling and growling that they were in great trouble.

As he spoke several of the beasts caught sight of him, and at once the great assemblage hushed as if by magic. The biggest of the tigers came up to the Lion and bowed, saying,

"Welcome, O King of Beasts! You have come in good time to fight our enemy and bring peace to all the animals of the forest once more."

"What is your trouble?" asked the Lion, quietly.

"We are all threatened," answered the tiger, "by a fierce enemy which has lately come into this forest. It is a most tremendous monster, like a great spider, with a body as big as an elephant and legs as long as a tree trunk. It has eight of these long legs, and as the monster crawls through the forest he seizes an animal with a leg and drags it to his mouth, where he eats it as a spider does a fly. Not one of us is safe while this fierce creature is alive, and we had called a meeting to decide how to take care of ourselves when you came among us."

The Lion thought for a moment.

"Are there any other lions in this forest?" he asked.

"No; there were some, but the monster has eaten them all. And, besides, they were none of them nearly so large and brave as you."

"If I put an end to your enemy will you bow down to me and obey me as King of the Forest?" enquired the Lion.

"We will do that gladly," returned the tiger; and all the other beasts roared with a mighty roar: "We will!"

"Where is this great spider of yours now?" asked the Lion.

"Yonder, among the oak trees," said the tiger, pointing with his forefoot."

"Take good care of these friends of mine," said the Lion, "and I will go at once to fight the monster."

He bade his comrades good-bye and marched proudly away to do battle with the enemy.

The great spider was lying asleep when the Lion found him, and it looked so ugly that its foe turned up his nose in disgust. Its legs were quite as long as the tiger had said, and it's body covered with coarse black hair. It had a great mouth, with a row of sharp teeth a foot long; but its head was joined to the pudgy body by a neck as slender as a wasp's waist. This gave the Lion a hint of the best way to attack the creature, and as he knew it was easier to fight it asleep than awake, he gave a great spring and landed directly upon the monster's back. Then, with one blow of his heavy paw, all armed with sharp claws, he knocked the spider's head from its body. Jumping down, he watched it until the long legs stopped wiggling, when he knew it was quite dead.

The Lion went back to the opening where the beasts of the forest were waiting for him and said, proudly,

"You need fear your enemy no longer."

Then the beasts bowed down to the Lion as their King, and he promised to come back and rule over them as soon as Dorothy was safely on her way to Kansas.

# Chapter XXII.
# The Country
# of the Quadlings

**T**he four travellers passed through the rest of the forest in safety, and when they came out from its gloom saw before them a steep hill, covered from top to bottom with great pieces of rock.

"That will be a hard climb," said the Scarecrow, "but we must get over the hill, nevertheless."

So he led the way and the others followed. They had nearly reached the first rock when they heard a rough voice cry out,

"Keep back!"

"Who are you?" asked the Scarecrow. Then a head showed itself over the rock and the same voice said,

"This hill belongs to us, and we don't allow anyone to cross it."

"But we must cross it," said the Scarecrow. "We're going to the country of the Quadlings."

"But you shall not!" replied the voice, and there stepped from behind the rock the strangest man the travellers had ever seen.

He was quite short and stout and had a big head, which was flat at the top and supported by a thick neck full of wrinkles. But he had no arms at all, and, seeing this, the Scarecrow did not fear that so helpless a creature could prevent them from climbing the hill. So he said,

"I'm sorry not to do as you wish, but we must pass over your hill whether you like it or not," and he walked boldly forward.

As quick as lightning the man's head shot forward and his neck stretched out until the top of the head, where it was flat, struck the Scarecrow in the middle and sent him tumbling, over and over, down the hill. Almost as quickly as it came the head went back to the body, and the man laughed harshly as he said,

"It isn't as easy as you think!"

A chorus of boisterous laughter came from the other rocks, and Dorothy saw hundreds of the armless Hammer-Heads upon the hillside, one behind every rock.

The Lion became quite angry at the laughter caused by the Scarecrow's mishap, and giving a loud roar that echoed like thunder he dashed up the hill.

Again a head shot swiftly out, and the great Lion went rolling down the hill as if he had been struck by a cannon ball.

Dorothy ran down and helped the Scarecrow to his feet, and the Lion came up to her, feeling rather bruised and sore, and said,

"It is useless to fight people with shooting heads; no one can withstand them."

"What can we do, then?" she asked.

"Call the Winged Monkeys," suggested the Tin Woodman; "you have still the right to command them once more."

"Very well," she answered, and putting on the Golden Cap she uttered the magic words. The Monkeys were as prompt as ever, and in a few moments the entire band stood before her.

"What are your commands?" enquired the King of the Monkeys, bowing low.

"Carry us over the hill to the country of the Quadlings," answered the girl.

"It shall be done," said the King, and at once the Winged Monkeys caught the four travellers and Toto up in their arms and flew away with them. As they passed over the hill the Hammer-Heads yelled with vexation, and shot their heads high in the air; but they could not reach the Winged Monkeys, which carried Dorothy and

*The head shot forward and struck the Scarecrow.*

her comrades safely over the hill and set them down in the beautiful country of the Quadlings.

"This is the last time you can summon us," said the leader to
Dorothy; "so good-bye and good luck to you."

"Good-bye, and thank you very much," returned the girl; and the
Monkeys rose into the air and were out of sight in a twinkling.

The country of the Quadlings seemed rich and happy. There
was field upon field of ripening grain, with well-paved roads running between, and pretty rippling brooks with strong bridges across
them. The fences and houses and bridges were all painted bright
red, just as they had been painted yellow in the country of the
Winkies and blue in the country of the Munchkins. The Quadlings
themselves, who were short and fat and looked chubby and good
natured, were dressed all in red, which showed bright against the
green grass and the yellowing grain.

The Monkeys had set them down near a farm house, and the
four travellers walked up to it and knocked at the door. It was
opened by the farmer's wife, and when Dorothy asked for something to eat the woman gave them all a good dinner, with three
kinds of cake and four kinds of cookies, and a bowl of milk for Toto.

"How far is it to the Castle of Glinda?" asked the child.

"It is not a great way," answered the farmer's wife. "Take the road
to the South and you will soon reach it."

Thanking the good woman, they started afresh and walked by the
fields and across the pretty bridges until they saw before them a very
beautiful Castle. Before the gates were three young girls, dressed in
handsome red uniforms trimmed with gold braid; and as Dorothy approached one of them said to her,

"Why have you come to the South Country?"

"To see the Good Witch who rules here," she answered. "Will
you take me to her?"

"Let me have your name and I will ask Glinda if she will receive
you." They told who they were, and the girl soldier went into the
Castle. After a few moments she came back to say that Dorothy and
the others were to be admitted at once.

# Chapter XXIII.
## The Good Witch Grants Dorothy's Wish.

# Before

they went to see Glinda, however, they were taken to a room of the Castle, where Dorothy washed her face and combed her hair, and the Lion shook the dust out of his mane, and the Scarecrow patted himself into his best shape, and the Woodman polished his tin and oiled his joints.

When they were all quite presentable they followed the soldier girl into a big room where the Witch Glinda sat upon a throne of rubies.

She was both beautiful and young to their eyes. Her hair was a rich red in color and fell in flowing ringlets over her shoulders. Her dress was pure white; but her eyes were blue,[44] and they looked kindly upon the little girl.

"What can I do for you, my child?" she asked.

Dorothy told the Witch all her story; how the cyclone had brought her to the Land of Oz, how she had found her companions, and of the wonderful adventures they had met with.

"My greatest wish now," she added, "is to get back to Kansas, for

Aunt Em will surely think something dreadful has happened to me, and that will make her put on mourning; and unless the crops are better this year than they were last I am sure Uncle Henry cannot afford it."

Glinda leaned forward and kissed the sweet, upturned face of the loving little girl.

"Bless your dear heart," she said, "I am sure I can tell you of a way to get back to Kansas." Then she added:

"But, if I do, you must give me the Golden Cap."

"Willingly!" exclaimed Dorothy; "indeed, it is of no use to me now, and when you have it you can command the Winged Monkeys three times."

"And I think I shall need their service just those three times," answered Glinda, smiling.

Dorothy then gave her the Golden Cap, and the Witch said to the Scarecrow,

"What will you do when Dorothy has left us?"

"I will return to the Emerald City," he replied, "for Oz has made me its ruler and the people like me. The only thing that worries me is how to cross the hill of the Hammer-Heads."

"By means of the Golden Cap I shall command the Winged Monkeys to carry you to the gates of the Emerald City," said Glinda, "for it would be a shame to deprive the people of so wonderful a ruler."

"Am I really wonderful?" asked the Scarecrow.

"You are unusual," replied Glinda.

Turning to the Tin Woodman, she asked:

"What will become of you when Dorothy leaves this country?"

He leaned on his axe and thought a moment. Then he said,

"The Winkies were very kind to me, and wanted me to rule over them after the Wicked Witch died. I am fond of the Winkies, and if I could get back again to the country of the West I should like nothing better than to rule over them forever."

"My second command to the Winged Monkeys," said Glinda, "will be that they carry you safely to the land of the Winkies. Your brains may not be so large to look at as those of the Scarecrow, but you are really brighter than he is—when you are well polished— and I am sure you will rule the Winkies wisely and well."

*"You must give me the Golden Cap."*

Then the Witch looked at the big, shaggy Lion and asked, "When Dorothy has returned to her own home, what will become of you?"

"Over the hill of the Hammer-Heads," he answered, "lies a grand old forest, and all the beasts that live there have made me their King. If I could only get back to this forest I would pass my life very happily there."

"My third command to the Winged Monkeys," said Glinda, "shall be to carry you to your forest. Then, having used up the powers of the Golden Cap, I shall give it to the King of the Monkeys, that he and his band may thereafter be free for evermore."

The Scarecrow and the Tin Woodman and the Lion now thanked the Good Witch earnestly for her kindness, and Dorothy exclaimed,

"You are certainly as good as you are beautiful! But you have not yet told me how to get back to Kansas."

"Your Silver Shoes will carry you over the desert," replied Glinda. "If you had known their power you could have gone back to your Aunt Em the very first day you came to this country."

"But then I should not have had my wonderful brains!" cried the Scarecrow. "I might have passed my whole life in the farmer's cornfield."

"And I should not have had my lovely heart," said the Tin Woodman. "I might have stood and rusted in the forest till the end of the world."

"And I should have lived a coward forever," declared the Lion, "and no beast in all the forest would have had a good word to say to me."

"This is all true," said Dorothy, "and I am glad I was of use to these good friends. But now that each of them has had what he most desired, and each is happy in having a kingdom to rule besides, I think I should like to go back to Kansas."

"The Silver Shoes," said the Good Witch, "have wonderful powers. And one of the most curious things about them is that they can carry you to any place in the world in three steps, and each step will be made in the wink of an eye. All you have to do is to knock the heels together three times and command the shoes to carry you wherever you wish to go."

"If that is so," said the child, joyfully, "I will ask them to carry me back to Kansas at once."

She threw her arms around the Lion's neck and kissed him, patting his big head tenderly. Then she kissed the Tin Woodman, who was weeping in a way most dangerous to his joints. But she hugged the soft, stuffed body of the Scarecrow in her arms instead of kissing his painted face, and found she was crying herself at this sorrowful parting from her loving comrades.

Glinda the Good stepped down from her ruby throne to give the little girl a good-bye kiss, and Dorothy thanked her for all the kindness she had shown to her friends and herself.

Dorothy now took Toto up solemnly in her arms, and having said one last good-bye she clapped the heels of her shoes together three times, saying,

"Take me home to Aunt Em!"

Instantly she was whirling through the air, so swiftly that all she could see or feel was the wind whistling past her ears.

The Silver Shoes took but three steps, and then she stopped so suddenly that she rolled over upon the grass several times before she knew where she was.

At length, however, she sat up and looked about her.

"Good gracious!" she cried.

For she was sitting on the broad Kansas prairie, and just before her was the new farm house Uncle Henry built after the cyclone had carried away the old one. Uncle Henry was milking the cows in the barnyard, and Toto had jumped out of her arms and was running toward the barn, barking joyously.

Dorothy stood up and found she was in her stocking-feet. For the Silver Shoes had fallen off in her flight through the air, and were lost forever in the desert.

# Home Again.

Aunt Em had just come out of the house to water the cabbages when she looked up and saw Dorothy running toward her.

"My darling child!" she cried, folding the little girl in her arms and covering her face with kisses; "where in the world did you come from?"

"From the Land of Oz," said Dorothy, gravely. "And here is Toto, too. And oh, Aunt Em! I'm so glad to be at home again!"

Here ends the story of "The Wonderful Wizard of Oz," which was written by L. Frank Baum and illustrated by William Wallace Denslow. The engravings were made by the Illinois Engraving Company, the paper was supplied by Dwight Bros. Paper Company, and Messrs. A. R. Barnes & Company printed the book for the publishers, the George M. Hill Company, completing it on the fifteenth day of May, in the year nineteen hundred.

# Endnotes

No commentary on *The Wonderful Wizard of Oz* is possible without Michael Patrick Hearn's indispensable annotated editions (1973, 2000) of *The Annotated Wizard of Oz: The Wonderful Wizard of Oz,* the latter edition of which I refer to amply here and in my introduction. I am also indebted to Katherine Rogers's *L. Frank Baum, Creator of Oz* and Michael O. Riley's *Oz and Beyond: The Fantasy World of L. Frank Baum,* for their informative backgrounds to the work and the author. See "For Further Reading" for full information on these titles.

1. (p. 14) *the house was as dull and gray as everything else:* In some form, the adjective "gray" appears ten times in the first six paragraphs to emphasize, by repetition, the aspect of home that Dorothy has sublimated but that the audience realizes is an essential element in her outlook.
2. (p. 14) *cyclone:* A *cyclone* is a storm system in which strong winds rotate around a center of low pressure. A *tropical cyclone* is a hurricane. In the midwestern United States, *cyclone* often means *tornado*; the two terms were interchangeable in Baum's day.
3. (p. 22) *on the dry gray prairies:* Oz announces its spectacular difference from Kansas instantly—with flowers, birds, and a river that murmuringly voices a greeting to Dorothy.
4. (p. 22) *the little woman's hat was white:* White is the witch color in Oz. Dorothy does not yet know it, but the Witch of the North is the little woman in the white dress in the company of the Munchkins.
5. (p. 23) *"But I thought all witches were wicked":* So did most of Baum's audience. The appearance of a good witch is unprecedented in children's literature and may have some bearing on Baum's acquaintance with theosophical beliefs and his apparent indifference to established religions.
6. (p. 27) *"The road to the City of Emeralds is paved with yellow brick":* While it is impossible to be certain about many of the elements in this story that at first appear to be symbolic, mixing the color of the road (yellow) and of the Munchkins (blue) yields green, the color of Dorothy's destination.
7. (p. 31) *It was gingham, with checks of white and blue:* The description of Dorothy's dress is interesting in that, while an American import into Oz, the colors of the dress include both Munchkin blue and

witch white, another suggestion that Dorothy lands in Oz to fulfill her destiny.

8. (p. 32) *as well as if they had been made for her:* The Cinderella touch of the Silver Shoes is another twist on a familiar detail. The Shoes are talismanic objects like the Golden Cap, which also "fitted her exactly" (page 135) and that she possesses once the Wicked Witch of the West is dead.

9. (p. 32) *the one paved with yellow brick:* The yellow brick road is one among many symbolic referents decoded by Littlefield in his famous analysis of *The Wizard of Oz* as a political allegory. See Henry M. Littlefield, "*The Wizard of Oz*: Parable on Populism," *American Quarterly* 1964 16:1, pp. 47–71.

10. (p. 50) *a man made entirely of tin:* Tin is not subject to rust, and in fact resists corrosion. Hearn (p. 135) reports that Russian versions of the novel describe the Woodman as made of iron.

11. (p. 53) *"the girl lived with an old woman":* The Tin Woodman fell in love with a girl whose story is consistent with those of distressed young maidens of fairy tales. The difference, of course, is Baum's indifference to the details of the romance and any erotic overtones that often play a subliminal role in the workings of fairy-tale plots.

12. (p. 63) *"It seems to me they must be more cowardly than you":* Dorothy, whom the audience will identify with, at times seems in on the authorial joke that is the center of the story: None of her companions actually lacks what he seeks. Despite her flatness as a literary character, Dorothy's approach reveals a core of common sense and confidence in the world around her.

13. (p. 67) *a tree full of nuts:* Was Dorothy originally a vegan? The only confirmed carnivore in the book is the Cowardly Lion, who takes his meals discreetly and always offstage. Dorothy's usual meal is nuts and fruit, and Toto at one point has milk. Another possible bit of evidence of the influence of Theosophy on Baum.

14. (p. 70) *Kalidahs:* There is no consensus about the origins of this nonce word, one of Baum's many verbal improvisations.

15. (p. 78) *the kind Stork:* The Stork, who always likes "to help anyone in trouble," represents one of those deputies of benign Nature who are legion in fairy tales and children's books, from the birds that communicate between Cinderella and her deceased mother to the robin that leads Mary Lennox to the gate of the secret garden. The Stork enunciates a principle that Dorothy repeats in her interview with the Wizard: The strength of the strong should always be in the service of the weak.

16. (p. 80) *lying fast asleep among the poppies:* There is nothing scientific or realistic about Baum's use of the poppy field. The scent of poppies does not cause sleepiness.

17. (p. 86) *"and obey his slightest wish":* One of the chapter's glaring anomalies concerns the behavior of the Tin Woodman, who cries over a crushed beetle and yet can slay a wildcat (and later forty wolves) without shedding a tear.

18. (p. 94) *"everything is green here":* The color-coordinated geography of Oz offers a tantalizing opportunity for students of the text to look for deeper meanings. The best summary of this, as usual, is given by Hearn, who demonstrates that the color scheme is consistent with color theory and with the positions of the primaries on the color wheel.

19. (p. 95) *brownie:* A brownie is a Scottish elf who secretly does children's chores and adults' housework. One of those indications of Baum's interaction with fairy-tale tradition is how he includes a traditional element and either reverses it (for example, a "good witch") or fuses it, at times oxymoronically (such as the humbug as wizard) with something of his own. Hearn also points out that the winged lady in the next chapter seems another borrowing from fairy-tale tradition.

20. (p. 96) *he could not speak:* Why can't Toto speak? In *The Wizard of Oz and Who He Was,* Gardner pointed out that Toto *does* speak in *Tik-Tok of Oz,* where according to the Sawhorse, "All animals talk" in Oz. In the last chapter Dorothy, who learns of this, coaxes Toto into speaking:

> "I've just learned, for the first time, that you can say words—if you want to. Don't you want to, Toto?"
>
> "Woof!" said Toto, and that meant "no."
>
> "Not just one word, Toto, to prove you're as good as any other animal in Oz?"
>
> "Woof!"
>
> "Just one word, Toto—and then you may run away."
>
> He looked at her steadily a moment.
>
> "All right. Here I go!" he said, and darted away as swift as an arrow.

21. (p. 105) *seven passages and up three flights of stairs:* Both seven and three are numbers that occur often in fantasy, where they may have a specific reference to numerology, but it is speculation to assume that Baum has any such connections in mind—here or elsewhere in the book.

22. (p. 105) *one of the prettiest gowns:* Dorothy changes from the blue-and-white gingham dress she put on in the land of the Munchkins.

23. (p. 106) *"I am Dorothy, the Small and Meek":* Note the capitalization, which calls attention to the Wizard's pompous identification of himself

as "Great and Terrible." Whether Dorothy intends her reply as modest mockery of the Wizard, the typography may be a tip-off that her author hardly takes his creation seriously.

**24.** (p. 108) *"Why should I do this for you?":* Compare page 78. Dorothy's power is moral, not physical or supernatural; she understands that the strength of the strong is or must always be in the service of the weak — an understanding that is the foundation of children's fantasy.

**25.** (p. 110) *"she needs a heart as much as the Tin Woodman":* The Scarecrow is resourceful but profoundly literal minded. His diagnosis of the Wizard's "defect" is another indicator that, for all three companions, thought is irony free.

**26.** (p. 117) *unlocked their spectacles:* This is an important detail that is easily overlooked, and it explains that Dorothy's green dress had become "pure white." The change is also interesting since white is the witch color.

**27.** (p. 119) *He seized his axe:* There is a stylistic elegance, a nearly scriptural simplicity, in this description of the Woodman's slaying the wolves. Hearn, in (p. 206, note 3), suggests the biblical echoes may be intentional.

**28.** (p. 120) *"This is my battle":* Again, this description is formulaic and reminiscent of many such moments in fairy tales.

**29.** (p. 123) *"she is protected by the Power of Good, and that is greater than the Power of Evil":* This is the prime directive of all fairy tales.

**30.** (p. 128) *no longer prisoners in a strange land:* This and several such details here and in the next chapter produce interesting parallels with the great deliverance narrative of Western literature, the book of Exodus. Dorothy and her companions are enslaved; water is an essential weapon in their deliverance; and the narrator self-consciously refers to herself and her friends as "prisoners in a strange land"; and the day of deliverance we learn will be commemorated by the Winkies "as a holiday, then and ever after" (p. 131).

**31.** (p. 135) *carry her sunbonnet in the basket:* This is the same pink sunbonnet Dorothy dons in chapter III (p. 31).

**32.** (p. 140) *the little whistle she had always carried about her neck:* Commentary is unable to explain this suddenly appearing accessory. The Wicked Witch used a whistle to summon the wolves, crows, and bees, but this is clearly not that whistle.

**33.** (p. 144) *"made us enslave the Winkies":* The story of Quelala and Gayelette supplies a thumbnail history of Oz geopolitics. The arrival of the Wizard from Omaha obviously would have preceded the showdown described here. Oz apparently had held the whole territory in his control until the Golden Cap inexplicably "fell into the hands of the Wicked Witch of the West," who used the Winged Monkeys to drive the Wizard from the West, which she then either repossessed or conquered, and to enslave the Winkies. See Hearn (p. 269, note 15) for his encapsulation.

34. (p. 148) *at four minutes after nine o'clock the next morning:* This is one among a handful of details that seem to be clues but that lead nowhere.

35. (p. 148) *He had once met the Winged Monkeys in the Land of the West:* A veiled reference to the Wizard's expulsion from the Land of the Winkies in chapter XIV (p. 144).

36. (p. 149) *"I am everywhere":* Is this a parody of the language of traditional Revelation (which features both a good deal of green as well as emerald)? There is little or no overt parody in *The Wonderful Wizard of Oz*—certainly nothing like what one finds in British children's fantasy of the period—and no vicious satire. On the other hand, Baum's theosophical interests and his gently dismissive attitude toward conventional religion may be at work here. Rogers points out his "personal interest in nontraditional religion and opposition to the organized churches" of his day (as well as his support of women's suffrage) is on record in the editorials that he wrote in 1890 and 1891 for the *Aberdeen Saturday Pioneer*, in which he advances the claims of Theosophy and at times sounds like a Jeffersonian Deist. See Rogers, *L. Frank Baum, Creator of Oz*, pp. 33–34.

37. (p. 150) *"I am Oz, the Great and Terrible," said the little man:* The scene of the Wizard's unmasking, one of the classic moments in American literature, inspired one of the most unforgettable lines in American cinema—"Pay no attention to the man behind the curtain!" Oz, like his creator (who sold dry goods at one point in his life), is at bottom a hardworking salesman.

38. (p. 153) *"and found the balloon floating over a strange and beautiful country":* The nearest precedent for a balloon ride that delivers its occupants to a land of mystery was Jules Verne's *Mysterious Island* (1874). Verne used balloon transport as well in *Five Weeks in a Balloon* (1863) and *Around the World in Eighty Days* (1873).

39. (p. 160) *"bran-new brains":* This is one of many examples of the puns that Baum loved so much. Hearn is terrific at tracking these down.

40. (p. 168) *"Hot air isn't as good as gas":* The earliest balloons used hot air, later replaced with gas, so the Wizard's knowledge is state-of-the-art in 1900.

41. (p. 176) *"Glinda is a beautiful woman":* This is Baum's second violation of traditional witch typology.

42. (p. 179) *"Attacked by the Fighting Trees":* Excepting the Fighting Trees, the 1939 MGM movie eliminated these last chapters, which include the help of the Winged Monkeys, the encounter with the

Hammer-Heads, and the visit to the country of the dainty china people. The fighting trees have a vague literary lineage. Every commentator points inevitably to Dante's Forest of the Suicides in *Inferno*, canto XIII, where sinners are translated into sentient vegetation that cries aloud when it is "wounded."

**43.** (p. 192) *he upset a china church with his tail and smashed it all to pieces:* In an interesting detail, the only object directly destroyed by the companions is a house of worship.

**44.** (p. 207) *Her hair was a rich red. . . . Her dress was pure white; but her eyes were blue:* An attentive reader, following the narrative's color codes, will probably react to the coincidence of a redheaded women with blue eyes in a white dress.

# Inspired by
## *The Wonderful Wizard of Oz*

### Sequels

L. Frank Baum wrote thirteen sequels to the original Oz tale, elaborating on the fantastic inhabitants of that enchanted land. He dedicated the first sequel, *The Marvelous Land of Oz* (1904), to David C. Montgomery and Fred A. Stone, the actors who played the Tin Woodman and the Scarecrow in Baum's successful musical *The Wizard of Oz* (discussed below). In *The Marvelous Land of Oz*, the Scarecrow, whom the Wizard named as his successor at the end of *The Wonderful Wizard of Oz*, enjoys his position as ruler of Oz. (The prominence of the Scarecrow in the 1904 book, which does not feature Dorothy, was most likely the result of his stage counterpart's great popularity.) Baum seems to have written *The Marvelous Land of Oz* with an eye toward stage adaptation: Part of the plot involves an army of women—easily imagined as high-kicking chorus girls—who challenge the Scarecrow's legitimacy. The plot's entanglements unwind at the hand of Glinda the Good Sorceress, who reveals that the young boy Tip is really Ozma, the rightful ruler of Oz, magically transformed into a boy by the wicked witch Mombi. Though the plot surprise may seem unorthodox, sex changes were familiar in popular theater of the day. Glinda then compels Mombi to restore Ozma to her true form.

Dorothy returns to the series in *Ozma of Oz* (1907), having aged about five years. She is whisked to Oz for the second time when she is washed overboard during a storm while on a voyage to Australia with Uncle Henry. She floats to land on a chicken coop, accompanied by a talking chicken, Billina. She meets Tik-Tok the mechanical clockwork man, and the vain Princess Langwidere, who, for variety's sake, wears a new head every day. Dorothy, with key assistance from Billina, eventually rescues Ozma and her band of friends, who had been transformed into decorative objects by the evil king of the nomes, Roquat of the Rock.

*Dorothy and the Wizard in Oz* (1908) reunites the heroine with the Wizard in an underground glass city. The remaining Oz books by Baum, which he continued writing until the end of his life, are *The Road to Oz* (1909), *The Emerald City of Oz* (1910), *The Patchwork Girl of Oz* (1913), *Tik-Tok of Oz* (1914), *The Scarecrow of Oz* (1915), *Rinkitink in Oz* (1916), *The Lost Princess of Oz* (1917), *The Tin Woodman of Oz* (1918), *The Magic of Oz* (1919), and *Glinda of Oz* (1920). Dorothy is not the main character but appears as one of the secondary characters in *The Patchwork Girl of Oz, The Lost Princess of Oz, The Tin Woodman of Oz,* and *The Magic of Oz.* She also appears at the ends of *Tik-Tok of Oz, The Scarecrow of Oz,* and *Rinkitink in Oz.* Baum's imaginative powers shine particularly in *The Emerald City of Oz* and in the final four novels. In addition to the novels, Baum created the Little Wizard Series, a collection of six short Oz tales, and *The Woggle-Bug Book,* a series of Sunday comics he wrote in 1904 and 1905.

After Baum's death, Ruth Plumly Thompson wrote nineteen Oz sequels, beginning with *The Royal Book of Oz* (1921) when Thompson was only twenty years old. After Thompson's run, John R. Neill wrote three Oz books. Neill had illustrated every Baum and Thompson Oz book except for the first, replacing W. W. Denslow after *The Wonderful Wizard of Oz.* After Neill's contributions, Jack Snow wrote two, Rachel Cosgrove wrote one, and Eloise McGraw and Lauren McGraw Wagner wrote one. The final Oz book, *The Laughing Dragon of Oz* (1934), was written by Baum's eldest son, Frank Joslyn Baum, who is better known for his biography of his father: *To Please a Child: A Biography of L. Frank Baum, Royal Historian of Oz* (1961).

## Theater

Inspired by the commercial success of *The Wonderful Wizard of Oz,* L. Frank Baum quickly adapted his novel for the stage. The 1902 musical comedy *The Wizard of Oz,* which replaced Toto with

Imogene the cow, was a popular success; it opened in Chicago, moved to Broadway, where it played for more than a year, and toured until 1911. A ten-minute silent film version of the play appeared in 1910; it was one of three films based on Baum's books to appear that year. The other two films were based on a combination of *The Marvelous Land of Oz* and *Dorothy and the Wizard in Oz* and the non-Oz story *John Dough and the Cherub*. Baum also wrote scripts and songs for two other Oz musicals. *The Woggle-Bug*, Baum's dramatization of *The Marvelous Land of Oz*, premiered in Chicago in 1905, soon after the novel's publication. The play, named after a giant professorial insect who roams Oz, ran for less than a month. It was followed in 1913 by the musical *The Tik-Tok Man of Oz*, which features Tik-Tok, Betsy Bobbin, and others from the books *Dorothy and the Wizard in Oz* and *The Road to Oz*, and plot elements Baum reused in the book *Tik-Tok of Oz*.

Baum's original story made a notable return to the Broadway stage in 1975 as *The Wiz*. The disco-infused musical comedy, which featured an all-black cast, won seven Tony Awards and ran for four years. The successful film version directed by Sidney Lumet, which appeared in 1978, starred Diana Ross as Dorothy, Michael Jackson as the Scarecrow, Lena Horne as Glinda the Good, and Richard Pryor as the eponymous Wiz.

A quarter century later, Oz made a splash on Broadway once again. Based on Gregory Maguire's best-selling novel *Wicked: The Life and Times of the Wicked Witch of the West* (1995), the musical *Wicked* opened in 2003 and won three Tony Awards. The intelligent, multilayered novel tells the life story of the Wicked Witch of the West, one of the most notorious villains in literature. Maguire's story humanizes the witch, whom he names Elphaba, by describing her difficult childhood as the only green-skinned girl at school. Raised by an alcoholic mother and plagued by her roommate Glinda, a shallow girl interested only in clothes and popularity, the studious Elphaba eventually sets out to overthrow the corrupt Wizard who has overtaken Oz. *Wicked* has the same ending as Baum's original tale, but in the retelling Maguire paints a vivid and sympathetic portrait of a well-developed character who is both fiery and appealing.

## Film

In the last century, more than one hundred feature and television films have been made based on Baum's Oz novels. Many of the earliest of these were spearheaded by Baum himself. Pursuing his interest in filmmaking, Baum co-produced *The Patchwork Girl of Oz* (1914), which was based on a popular Oz sequel and was made by Baum's Oz Film Manufacturing Company. The company was also responsible for *The Magic Cloak of Oz* (1914; released in 1917) and *His Majesty, the Scarecrow of Oz* (1914). In 1925 Baum's son Frank Joslyn Baum co-wrote the screenplay with director Leon Lee for *The Wizard of Oz*, a film that features Oliver Hardy as the Tin Woodman.

But the release of the 1939 film *The Wizard of Oz*—a work that has in many ways eclipsed Baum's novel in the cultural consciousness—changed everything. It has been said that more people have seen *The Wizard of Oz* than any other movie. Its magnificence and impact are even more surprising given the difficulty of producing the film. Nominally directed by Victor Fleming, *Wizard* required a clutch of directors to save it from disaster. The original director, Richard Thorpe, was fired after twelve days of shooting, and the legendary George Cukor did not last a week. Though Fleming shot the bulk of the picture, King Vidor took over near the end of the process to film the Kansas sequences, including the famous "Somewhere Over the Rainbow" scene, which was nearly cut from the film. Salmon Rushdie, in his seminal study of the film, writes "Who, then, is the *auteur* of *The Wizard of Oz*? No single writer can claim that honour, not even the author of the original book." Indeed, the screenplay was penned by Noel Langley, Florence Ryerson, and Edgar Allan Woolf, as well as a host of uncredited writers.

Serendipitously, however, *The Wizard of Oz* is near perfect, in part due to sixteen-year-old Judy Garland's star-making turn as Dorothy Gale, the ebullient score, which features "Ding Dong! The Witch Is Dead," "Follow the Yellow Brick Road," and "We're Off to See the Wizard," and a wonderfully creative adaptation of Baum's original ideas. For example, in the film Oz is a dream place to which Dorothy travels while unconscious. The Tin Man, the Scarecrow, and the Cowardly Lion all correlate to farmhands employed by Auntie Em, and the Wizard himself is an alchemized Professor Marvel, whom Dorothy had met on his travels through Kansas. And, in a stroke of cinematic genius, it was decided to shoot the Kansas scenes that frame the film in black and white—actually in a drab, sepia tint—and the Oz sequences in brilliant Technicolor. At the time of the film's production, nearly all films were still shot in black and white, so this shift to color as Dorothy enters the enchanted realm of Oz would have had an extraordinary impact on audiences.

Called the greatest year in American cinema, 1939 saw the appearance of a host of films now considered classics, including *Mr. Smith Goes to Washington*, *Stagecoach*, *Wuthering Heights*, and *Gone with the Wind*, which was also directed by Fleming and which dominated the Academy Awards that year. But *Wizard* won two Oscars in the musical categories: Original Score and Best Song for "Over the Rainbow," with music by Harold Arlen and lyrics by E. Y. Harburg. Additionally, Judy Garland picked up a special Oscar "for her outstanding performance as a screen juvenile during the past year."

*The Wizard of Oz* has become one of America's most important contributions to cinema, as well as an exemplar to which filmmakers consistently allude. For instance, when adapting Barry Gifford's novel *Wild at Heart* for his film of the same name (1990), David Lynch imposed a *Wizard of Oz* structure—replete with a cackling witch and a snakeskin jacket standing in for the Silver Shoes/Ruby Slippers—to give the story a happy ending. This same fidelity of audiences to 1939's *Wizard* has doomed all subsequent attempts at Oz sequels.

Disney's *Return to Oz* (1985), directed by Oscar-winning editor Walter Murch, is a competent, ambitious rendition of Baum's novels *The Marvelous Land of Oz* and *Ozma of Oz*. *Return to Oz* features spectacular visuals, which, though invidious comparisons to *Wizard* are inevitably made, bear the stamp of W. W. Denslow's original book illustrations. Starring Piper Laurie as Auntie Em and Fairuza Balk in her debut role as Dorothy,

Murch's film parades a slew of characters, including the artfully realized Tik-Tok; the sweet Jack Pumpkinhead; and the hunched-over Wheelers, whose terrifying, squeaking wheels always precede them on screen.

# Comments & Questions

*In this section, we aim to provide the reader with an array of perspectives on the text, as well as questions that challenge those perspectives. The commentary has been culled from sources as diverse as reviews contemporaneous with the work, letters written by the author, literary criticism of later generations, and appreciations written throughout the work's history. Following the commentary, a series of questions seeks to filter L. Frank Baum's* The Wonderful Wizard of Oz *through a variety of points of view and bring about a richer understanding of this enduring work.*

## Comments

**NEW YORK TIMES**

It is impossible to conceive of a greater contrast than exists between the children's books of antiquity that were new publications during the sixteenth century and modern children's books of which "The Wonderful Wizard of Oz" is typical. The crudeness that was characteristic of the old-time publications that were intended for the delectation and amusement of ancestral children would now be enough to cause the modern child to yell with rage and vigor and to instantly reject the offending volume, if not to throw it out of the window. The time when anything was considered good enough for children has long since passed, and the volumes devoted to our youth are based upon the fact that they are the future citizens: that they are the country's hope, and are thus worthy of the best, not the worst, that art can give. . . . In "The Wonderful Wizard of Oz" the fact is clearly recognized that the young as well as their elders love novelty. They are pleased with dashes of color and something new in place of the old, familiar, and winged fairies of Grimm and Andersen.

—September 8, 1900

**BOSTON REVIEW**

Under the sweet simplicity of the tale for children is a satiric allegory on modern history for big people. The Scarecrow wears a Russian blouse, the fierce Tin Woodman bears a striking resemblance to Emperor Wilhelm of Germany, the Cowardly Lion with its scarlet beard and tail tip at once suggest Great Britain, and the Flying Monkeys wear a military cap in Spanish colors.

—from a review of *The Wonderful Wizard of Oz*
(September 29, 1900)

**EDWARD WAGENKNECHT**

It is in *The Wizard of Oz* that we meet the first distinctive attempt to construct a fairyland out of American materials. Baum's long series of Oz books represents thus an important pioneering work: they may even be considered an American utopia.

—from *Utopia Americana* (1929)

**HENRY M. LITTLEFIELD**

*The Wizard of Oz* says so much about so many things that it is hard not to imagine a satisfied and mischievous gleam in Lyman Frank Baum's eye as he had Dorothy say, "And oh, Aunt Em! I'm so glad to be at home again!"

—from "The Wizard of Oz: Parable on Populism,"
*American Quarterly* (Spring 1964)

**MARTIN GARDNER**

It is entirely possible that 500 years from now citizens of the earth, studying 20th-century children's literature, will know of Kansas only because Dorothy Gale once lived there.

—from the *New York Times Book Review* (May 2, 1971)

**GORE VIDAL**

I could not stop reading and rereading [*The Emerald City of Oz*]. But "reading" is not the right word. In some mysterious way, I was translating myself to Oz, a place which I was to inhabit for many years while, simultaneously, visiting other fictional worlds as well as

maintaining my cover in that dangerous one known as "real." With
*The Emerald City,* I became addicted to reading.

—from the *New York Review of Books* (September 19, 1977)

SALMAN RUSHDIE

*The Wizard of Oz* is a film whose driving force is the inadequacy
of adults, even of good adults, and how the weakness of grown-ups
forces children to take control of their own destinies, and so, ironi-
cally, grow up themselves. The journey from Kansas to Oz is a rite
of passage from a world in which Dorothy's parent-substitutes, Auntie Em and Uncle Henry, are powerless to help her save her dog
Toto from the marauding Miss Gulch, into a world where the people are her own size, and in which she is never, ever treated as a
child but as a heroine.

—from *The Wizard of Oz* (1992)

JOHN UPDIKE

*Oz* is too unearthly to carry much political punch. It is constructed
not of revolutionary intent but of wishful thinking.

—from the *New Yorker* (September 25, 2000)

## Questions

1. Is *The Wonderful Wizard of Oz* the kind of work in which one
can legitimately extract psychological or allegorical meanings?
Should the Scarecrow, the Cowardly Lion, and the Tin Woodman
be understood as three aspects of human personality?

2. J. T. Barberese describes *Oz* as "the first American children's
book." What is noticeably or even strikingly "American" about it?
How would a book like *Alice's Adventures in Wonderland* not be
"American"?

3. *Oz* has the form of a quest narrative—a hero or heroine sets out
to find or do something definitive. Usually the hero or heroine does

do or find something that will from that point forward give meaning to his or her life, but that which is found or accomplished is seldom what was expected. Is Dorothy on a quest? Is her quest successful? If so, what was the quest for? What did she, in fact, gain from it in the end?

# For Further Reading

## The Oz Series

BY L. FRANK BAUM

*The Wonderful Wizard of Oz.* Illustrated by W. W. Denslow. Chicago and New York: George M. Hill, 1900.

*The Marvelous Land of Oz.* Illustrated by John R. Neill. Chicago: Reilly and Britton, 1904.

*Ozma of Oz.* Illustrated by John R. Neill. Chicago: Reilly and Britton, 1907.

*Dorothy and the Wizard in Oz.* Illustrated by John R. Neill. Chicago: Reilly and Britton, 1908.

*The Road to Oz.* Illustrated by John R. Neill. Chicago: Reilly and Britton, 1909.

*The Emerald City of Oz.* Illustrated by John R. Neill. Chicago: Reilly and Britton, 1910.

*The Patchwork Girl of Oz.* Illustrated by John R. Neill. Chicago: Reilly and Britton, 1913.

*The Little Wizard Series: The Cowardly Lion and the Hungry Tiger, Little Dorothy and Toto, Tiktok and the Nome King, Ozma and the Little Wizard, Jack Pumpkinhead and the Sawhorse,* and *The Scarecrow and the Tin Woodman,* 1913. Reissued in a single volume, *Little Wizard Stories of Oz.* Illustrated by John R. Neill. Chicago: Reilly and Britton, 1914.

*Tik-Tok of Oz.* Illustrated by John R. Neill. Chicago: Reilly and Britton, 1914.

*The Scarecrow of Oz.* Illustrated by John R. Neill. Chicago: Reilly and Britton, 1915.

*Rinkitink in Oz.* Illustrated by John R. Neill. Chicago: Reilly and Britton, 1916.

*The Lost Princess of Oz.* Illustrated by John R. Neill. Chicago: Reilly and Britton, 1917.

*The Tin Woodman of Oz.* Illustrated by John R. Neill. Chicago: Reilly and Britton, 1918.

*The Magic of Oz.* Illustrated by John R. Neill. Chicago: Reilly and Lee, 1919.

*Glinda of Oz.* Illustrated by John R. Neill. Chicago: Reilly and Lee, 1920.

**BY RUTH PLUMLY THOMPSON, ALL ILLUSTRATED BY JOHN R. NEILL**

*The Royal Book of Oz.* Chicago: Reilly and Lee, 1921. Published under Baum's name but written by Thompson.

*Kabumpo in Oz.* Chicago: Reilly and Lee, 1922.

*The Cowardly Lion of Oz.* Chicago: Reilly and Lee, 1923.

*Grampa in Oz.* Chicago: Reilly and Lee, 1924.

*The Lost King of Oz.* Chicago: Reilly and Lee, 1925.

*The Hungry Tiger of Oz.* Chicago: Reilly and Lee, 1926.

*The Gnome King of Oz.* Chicago: Reilly and Lee, 1927.

*The Giant Horse of Oz.* Chicago and New York: Reilly and Lee, 1928.

*Jack Pumpkinhead of Oz.* Chicago and New York: Reilly and Lee, 1929.

*The Yellow Knight of Oz.* Chicago and New York: Reilly and Lee, 1930.

*Pirates in Oz.* Chicago: Reilly and Lee, 1931.

*The Purple Prince of Oz.* Chicago: Reilly and Lee, 1932.

*Ojo in Oz.* Chicago: Reilly and Lee, 1933.

*Speedy in Oz.* Chicago: Reilly and Lee, 1934.

*The Wishing Horse of Oz.* Chicago: Reilly and Lee, 1935.

*Captain Salt in Oz.* Chicago: Reilly and Lee, 1936.

*Handy Mandy in Oz.* Chicago: Reilly and Lee, 1937.

*The Silver Princess in Oz.* Chicago: Reilly and Lee, 1938.

*Ozoplaning with the Wizard of Oz.* Chicago: Reilly and Lee, 1939.

**BY FRANK JOSLYN BAUM**

*The Laughing Dragon of Oz.* Illustrated by Milt Younger. Racine, WI: Whitman Publishing, 1934.

**WRITTEN AND ILLUSTRATED BY JOHN R. NEILL**

*The Wonder City of Oz.* Chicago: Reilly and Lee, 1940.

*The Scalawagons of Oz.* Chicago: Reilly and Lee, 1941.

*Lucky Bucky in Oz.* Chicago: Reilly and Lee, 1942.

**BY JACK SNOW**
*The Magical Mimics in Oz*. Illustrated by Frank Kramer. Chicago: Reilly and Lee, 1946.
*The Shaggy Man of Oz*. Illustrated by Frank Kramer. Chicago: Reilly and Lee, 1949.

**BY RACHEL R. COSGROVE**
*The Hidden Valley of Oz*. Illustrated by Dirk [Dirk Gringhuis]. Chicago: Reilly and Lee, 1951.

**BY ELOISE JARVIS MCGRAW AND LAUREN MCGRAW WAGER**
*Merry Go Round in Oz*. Illustrated by Dick Martin. Chicago: Reilly and Lee, 1963.

## An Oz Bibliography

Baum, Frank Joslyn, and Russell P. MacFall. *To Please a Child: A Biography of L. Frank Baum, Royal Historian of Oz*. Chicago: Reilly and Lee, 1961.

Baum, L. Frank. *The Wizard of Oz*. Pictures by W. W. Denslow. Edited by Michael Patrick Hearn. New York: Schocken Books, 1983.

Cashdan, Sheldon. *The Witch Must Die: How Fairy Tales Shape Our Lives*. New York: Basic Books, 1999.

Dighe, Ranjit S., ed. *The Historian's Wizard of Oz: Reading L. Frank Baum's Classic as a Political and Monetary Allegory*. Westport, CT, and London: Praeger, 2002.

Gardner, Martin, and Russel B. Nye. *The Wizard of Oz and Who He Was*. East Lansing: Michigan State University Press, 1957.

Hanff, Peter E., and Douglas G. Greene. *Bibliographia Oziana: A Concise Bibliographical Checklist of the Oz Books by L. Frank Baum and His Successors*. Kinderhook, IL: International Wizard of Oz Club, 1976.

Harmetz, Aljean. *The Making of "The Wizard of Oz."* Introduction by Margaret Hamilton. New York: Alfred A. Knopf, 1977.

Hearn, Michael Patrick, ed. *The Annotated Wizard of Oz : The Wonderful Wizard of Oz*. Pictures by W. W. Denslow. Introduction, notes, and bibliography by Michael Patrick Hearn. New York: Clarkson N. Potter, 1973. Revised edition, with a preface by Martin Gardner. New York: Norton, 2000.

Huebel, Harry Russell, compiler. *Things in the Driver's Seat: Readings in Popular Culture.* Chicago: Rand McNally, 1972. Contains Henry M. Littlefield's essay "*The Wizard of Oz*: Parable on Populism."

Langley, Noel, Florence Ryerson, and Edgar Allan Woolf. *The Wizard of Oz: The Screenplay.* Edited and with an introduction by Michael Patrick Hearn. New York: Delta Books, 1989.

Nathanson, Paul. *Over the Rainbow: The Wizard of Oz as a Secular Myth of America.* Albany: State University of New York Press, 1991.

Riley, Michael O. *Oz and Beyond: The Fantasy World of L. Frank Baum.* Lawrence: University Press of Kansas, 1997.

Rogers, Katharine M. *L. Frank Baum, Creator of Oz.* New York: St. Martin's Press, 2002.

Rushdie, Salman. *The Wizard of Oz.* London: BFI, 1992.

Swartz, Mark Evan. *Oz Before the Rainbow: L. Frank Baum's The Wonderful Wizard of Oz on Stage and Screen to 1939.* Baltimore, MD: Johns Hopkins University Press, 2000.

Look for the following titles, available now from
# BARNES & NOBLE CLASSICS

Visit your local bookstore for these and more fine titles.
Or to order online go to: WWW.BN.COM/CLASSICS

| Title | Author | ISBN | Price |
|---|---|---|---|
| Adventures of Huckleberry Finn | Mark Twain | 1-59308-112-X | $5.95 |
| The Adventures of Tom Sawyer | Mark Twain | 1-59308-139-1 | $5.95 |
| The Aeneid | Vergil | 1-59308-237-1 | $7.95 |
| Aesop's Fables | | 1-59308-062-X | $5.95 |
| The Age of Innocence | Edith Wharton | 1-59308-143-X | $5.95 |
| Agnes Grey | Anne Brontë | 1-59308-323-8 | $6.95 |
| Alice's Adventures in Wonderland and Through the Looking-Glass | Lewis Carroll | 1-59308-015-8 | $5.95 |
| Anna Karenina | Leo Tolstoy | 1-59308-027-1 | $8.95 |
| The Arabian Nights | Anonymous | 1-59308-281-9 | $9.95 |
| The Art of War | Sun Tzu | 1-59308-017-4 | $7.95 |
| The Autobiography of an Ex-Colored Man and Other Writings | James Weldon Johnson | 1-59308-289-4 | $5.95 |
| The Awakening and Selected Short Fiction | Kate Chopin | 1-59308-113-8 | $6.95 |
| Babbitt | Sinclair Lewis | 1-59308-267-3 | $7.95 |
| The Beautiful and Damned | F. Scott Fitzgerald | 1-59308-245-2 | $7.95 |
| Beowulf | Anonymous | 1-59308-266-5 | $4.95 |
| Billy Budd and The Piazza Tales | Herman Melville | 1-59308-253-3 | $5.95 |
| Bleak House | Charles Dickens | 1-59308-311-4 | $9.95 |
| The Bostonians | Henry James | 1-59308-297-5 | $8.95 |
| The Brothers Karamazov | Fyodor Dostoevsky | 1-59308-045-X | $9.95 |
| Bulfinch's Mythology | Thomas Bulfinch | 1-59308-273-8 | $12.95 |
| The Call of the Wild and White Fang | Jack London | 1-59308-200-2 | $5.95 |
| Candide | Voltaire | 1-59308-028-X | $4.95 |
| The Canterbury Tales | Geoffrey Chaucer | 1-59308-080-8 | $9.95 |
| A Christmas Carol, The Chimes and The Cricket on the Hearth | Charles Dickens | 1-59308-033-6 | $5.95 |
| The Collected Oscar Wilde | | 1-59308-310-6 | $9.95 |
| The Collected Poems of Emily Dickinson | | 1-59308-050-6 | $5.95 |
| Common Sense and Other Writings | Thomas Paine | 1-59308-209-6 | $6.95 |
| The Communist Manifesto and Other Writings | Karl Marx and Friedrich Engels | 1-59308-100-6 | $5.95 |
| The Complete Sherlock Holmes, Vol. I | Sir Arthur Conan Doyle | 1-59308-034-4 | $7.95 |
| The Complete Sherlock Holmes, Vol. II | Sir Arthur Conan Doyle | 1-59308-040-9 | $7.95 |
| Confessions | Saint Augustine | 1-59308-259-2 | $6.95 |
| A Connecticut Yankee in King Arthur's Court | Mark Twain | 1-59308-210-X | $7.95 |
| The Count of Monte Cristo | Alexandre Dumas | 1-59308-151-0 | $7.95 |
| The Country of the Pointed Firs and Selected Short Fiction | Sarah Orne Jewett | 1-59308-262-2 | $7.95 |
| Crime and Punishment | Fyodor Dostoevsky | 1-59308-081-6 | $8.95 |
| Daisy Miller and Washington Square | Henry James | 1-59308-105-7 | $4.95 |
| Daniel Deronda | George Eliot | 1-59308-290-8 | $8.95 |
| Dead Souls | Nikolai Gogol | 1-59308-092-1 | $7.95 |

(continued)

| Title | Author | ISBN | Price |
|---|---|---|---|
| The Deerslayer | James Fenimore Cooper | 1-59308-211-8 | $7.95 |
| Don Quixote | Miguel de Cervantes | 1-59308-046-8 | $9.95 |
| Dracula | Bram Stoker | 1-59308-114-6 | $6.95 |
| Emma | Jane Austen | 1-59308-152-9 | $6.95 |
| Essays and Poems by Ralph Waldo Emerson | | 1-59308-076-X | $6.95 |
| Essential Dialogues of Plato | | 1-59308-269-X | $9.95 |
| The Essential Tales and Poems of Edgar Allan Poe | | 1-59308-064-6 | $7.95 |
| Ethan Frome and Selected Stories | Edith Wharton | 1-59308-090-5 | $5.95 |
| Fairy Tales | Hans Christian Andersen | 1-59308-260-6 | $9.95 |
| Far from the Madding Crowd | Thomas Hardy | 1-59308-223-1 | $7.95 |
| The Federalist | Hamilton, Madison, Jay | 1-59308-282-7 | $7.95 |
| Founding America: Documents from the Revolution to the Bill of Rights | Jefferson, et al. | 1-59308-230-4 | $9.95 |
| Frankenstein | Mary Shelley | 1-59308-115-4 | $4.95 |
| The Good Soldier | Ford Madox Ford | 1-59308-268-1 | $6.95 |
| Great American Short Stories: From Hawthorne to Hemingway | Various | 1-59308-086-7 | $7.95 |
| The Great Escapes: Four Slave Narratives | Various | 1-59308-294-0 | $6.95 |
| Great Expectations | Charles Dickens | 1-59308-116-2 | $6.95 |
| Grimm's Fairy Tales | Jacob and Wilhelm Grimm | 1-59308-056-5 | $7.95 |
| Gulliver's Travels | Jonathan Swift | 1-59308-132-4 | $5.95 |
| Hard Times | Charles Dickens | 1-59308-156-1 | $5.95 |
| Heart of Darkness and Selected Short Fiction | Joseph Conrad | 1-59308-123-5 | $5.95 |
| The History of the Peloponnesian War | Thucydides | 1-59308-091-3 | $9.95 |
| The House of Mirth | Edith Wharton | 1-59308-153-7 | $6.95 |
| The House of the Dead and Poor Folk | Fyodor Dostoevsky | 1-59308-194-4 | $7.95 |
| The House of the Seven Gables | Nathaniel Hawthorne | 1-59308-231-2 | $7.95 |
| The Hunchback of Notre Dame | Victor Hugo | 1-59308-140-5 | $7.95 |
| The Idiot | Fyodor Dostoevsky | 1-59308-058-1 | $7.95 |
| The Iliad | Homer | 1-59308-232-0 | $7.95 |
| The Importance of Being Earnest and Four Other Plays | Oscar Wilde | 1-59308-059-X | $6.95 |
| Incidents in the Life of a Slave Girl | Harriet Jacobs | 1-59308-283-5 | $5.95 |
| The Inferno | Dante Alighieri | 1-59308-051-4 | $6.95 |
| The Interpretation of Dreams | Sigmund Freud | 1-59308-298-3 | $8.95 |
| Ivanhoe | Sir Walter Scott | 1-59308-246-0 | $7.95 |
| Jane Eyre | Charlotte Brontë | 1-59308-117-0 | $7.95 |
| Journey to the Center of the Earth | Jules Verne | 1-59308-252-5 | $4.95 |
| Jude the Obscure | Thomas Hardy | 1-59308-035-2 | $6.95 |
| The Jungle Books | Rudyard Kipling | 1-59308-109-X | $5.95 |
| The Jungle | Upton Sinclair | 1-59308-118-9 | $6.95 |
| King Solomon's Mines | H. Rider Haggard | 1-59308-275-4 | $4.95 |
| Lady Chatterley's Lover | D. H. Lawrence | 1-59308-239-8 | $6.95 |
| The Last of the Mohicans | James Fenimore Cooper | 1-59308-137-5 | $5.95 |
| Leaves of Grass: First and "Death-bed" Editions | Walt Whitman | 1-59308-083-2 | $9.95 |
| The Legend of Sleepy Hollow and Other Writings | Washington Irving | 1-59308-225-8 | $6.95 |
| Les Misérables | Victor Hugo | 1-59308-066-2 | $9.95 |
| Les Liaisons Dangereuses | Pierre Choderlos de Laclos | 1-59308-240-1 | $7.95 |
| Little Women | Louisa May Alcott | 1-59308-108-1 | $6.95 |
| Lost Illusions | Honoré de Balzac | 1-59308-315-7 | $9.95 |

(continued)

| | | | |
|---|---|---|---|
| Madame Bovary | Gustave Flaubert | 1-59308-052-2 | $6.95 |
| Maggie: A Girl of the Streets and Other Writings about New York | Stephen Crane | 1-59308-248-7 | $6.95 |
| The Magnificent Ambersons | Booth Tarkington | 1-59308-263-0 | $7.95 |
| Main Street | Sinclair Lewis | 1-59308-386-6 | $8.95 |
| Man and Superman and Three Other Plays | George Bernard Shaw | 1-59308-067-0 | $7.95 |
| The Man in the Iron Mask | Alexandre Dumas | 1-59308-233-9 | $9.95 |
| Mansfield Park | Jane Austen | 1-59308-154-5 | $5.95 |
| The Mayor of Casterbridge | Thomas Hardy | 1-59308-309-2 | $5.95 |
| The Metamorphoses | Ovid | 1-59308-276-2 | $7.95 |
| The Metamorphosis and Other Stories | Franz Kafka | 1-59308-029-8 | $6.95 |
| Moby-Dick | Herman Melville | 1-59308-018-2 | $9.95 |
| Moll Flanders | Daniel Defoe | 1-59308-216-9 | $6.95 |
| My Ántonia | Willa Cather | 1-59308-202-9 | $5.95 |
| My Bondage and My Freedom | Frederick Douglass | 1-59308-301-7 | $6.95 |
| Narrative of Sojourner Truth | | 1-59308-293-2 | $6.95 |
| Narrative of the Life of Frederick Douglass, an American Slave | | 1-59308-041-7 | $4.95 |
| Nicholas Nickleby | Charles Dickens | 1-59308-300-9 | $8.95 |
| Night and Day | Virginia Woolf | 1-59308-212-6 | $7.95 |
| Nostromo | Joseph Conrad | 1-59308-193-6 | $7.95 |
| Notes from Underground, The Double and Other Stories | Fyodor Dostoevsky | 1-59308-124-3 | $7.95 |
| O Pioneers! | Willa Cather | 1-59308-205-3 | $5.95 |
| The Odyssey | Homer | 1-59308-009-3 | $5.95 |
| Of Human Bondage | W. Somerset Maugham | 1-59308-238-X | $9.95 |
| Oliver Twist | Charles Dickens | 1-59308-206-1 | $6.95 |
| The Origin of Species | Charles Darwin | 1-59308-077-8 | $7.95 |
| Paradise Lost | John Milton | 1-59308-095-6 | $7.95 |
| The Paradiso | Dante Alighieri | 1-59308-317-3 | $8.95 |
| Père Goriot | Honoré de Balzac | 1-59308-285-1 | $8.95 |
| Persuasion | Jane Austen | 1-59308-130-8 | $5.95 |
| Peter Pan | J. M. Barrie | 1-59308-213-4 | $4.95 |
| The Phantom of the Opera | Gaston Leroux | 1-59308-249-5 | $6.95 |
| The Picture of Dorian Gray | Oscar Wilde | 1-59308-025-5 | $4.95 |
| The Pilgrim's Progress | John Bunyan | 1-59308-254-1 | $7.95 |
| A Portrait of the Artist as a Young Man and Dubliners | James Joyce | 1-59308-031-X | $6.95 |
| The Possessed | Fyodor Dostoevsky | 1-59308-250-9 | $9.95 |
| Pride and Prejudice | Jane Austen | 1-59308-201-0 | $6.95 |
| The Prince and Other Writings | Niccolò Machiavelli | 1-59308-060-3 | $5.95 |
| The Prince and the Pauper | Mark Twain | 1-59308-218-5 | $4.95 |
| Pudd'nhead Wilson and Those Extraordinary Twins | Mark Twain | 1-59308-255-X | $6.95 |
| The Purgatorio | Dante Alighieri | 1-59308-219-3 | $8.95 |
| Pygmalion and Three Other Plays | George Bernard Shaw | 1-59308-078-6 | $7.95 |
| The Red Badge of Courage and Selected Short Fiction | Stephen Crane | 1-59308-119-7 | $4.95 |
| Republic | Plato | 1-59308-097-2 | $6.95 |
| The Return of the Native | Thomas Hardy | 1-59308-220-7 | $7.95 |
| Robinson Crusoe | Daniel Defoe | 1-59308-360-2 | $5.95 |
| A Room with a View | E. M. Forster | 1-59308-288-6 | $5.95 |
| Scaramouche | Rafael Sabatini | 1-59308-242-8 | $7.95 |
| The Scarlet Letter | Nathaniel Hawthorne | 1-59308-207-X | $5.95 |

(continued)

| | | | |
|---|---|---|---|
| **The Scarlet Pimpernel** | Baroness Orczy | 1-59308-234-7 | $5.95 |
| **The Secret Agent** | Joseph Conrad | 1-59308-305-X | $6.95 |
| **The Secret Garden** | Frances Hodgson Burnett | 1-59308-277-0 | $5.95 |
| **Selected Stories of O. Henry** | | 1-59308-042-5 | $5.95 |
| **Sense and Sensibility** | Jane Austen | 1-59308-125-1 | $5.95 |
| **Siddhartha** | Hermann Hesse | 1-59308-379-3 | $5.95 |
| **Silas Marner and Two Short Stories** | George Eliot | 1-59308-251-7 | $6.95 |
| **Sister Carrie** | Theodore Dreiser | 1-59308-226-6 | $8.95 |
| **The Souls of Black Folk** | W. E. B. Du Bois | 1-59308-014-X | $5.95 |
| **The Strange Case of Dr. Jekyll and Mr. Hyde and Other Stories** | Robert Louis Stevenson | 1-59308-131-6 | $4.95 |
| **Swann's Way** | Marcel Proust | 1-59308-295-9 | $8.95 |
| **A Tale of Two Cities** | Charles Dickens | 1-59308-138-3 | $5.95 |
| **Tarzan of the Apes** | Edgar Rice Burroughs | 1-59308-227-4 | $6.95 |
| **Tess of d'Urbervilles** | Thomas Hardy | 1-59308-228-2 | $7.95 |
| **This Side of Paradise** | F. Scott Fitzgerald | 1-59308-243-6 | $6.95 |
| **Three Theban Plays** | Sophocles | 1-59308-235-5 | $6.95 |
| **Thus Spoke Zarathustra** | Friedrich Nietzsche | 1-59308-278-9 | $7.95 |
| **The Time Machine and The Invisible Man** | H. G. Wells | 1-59308-388-2 | $6.95 |
| **Tom Jones** | Henry Fielding | 1-59308-070-0 | $8.95 |
| **Treasure Island** | Robert Louis Stevenson | 1-59308-247-9 | $4.95 |
| **The Turn of the Screw, The Aspern Papers and Two Stories** | Henry James | 1-59308-043-3 | $5.95 |
| **Twenty Thousand Leagues Under the Sea** | Jules Verne | 1-59308-302-5 | $5.95 |
| **Uncle Tom's Cabin** | Harriet Beecher Stowe | 1-59308-121-9 | $7.95 |
| **Vanity Fair** | William Makepeace Thackeray | 1-59308-071-9 | $7.95 |
| **The Varieties of Religious Experience** | William James | 1-59308-072-7 | $7.95 |
| **Villette** | Charlotte Brontë | 1-59308-316-5 | $9.95 |
| **The Virginian** | Owen Wister | 1-59308-236-3 | $7.95 |
| **Walden and Civil Disobedience** | Henry David Thoreau | 1-59308-208-8 | $5.95 |
| **War and Peace** | Leo Tolstoy | 1-59308-073-5 | $12.95 |
| **The War of the Worlds** | H. G. Wells | 1-59308-362-9 | $5.95 |
| **Ward No. 6 and Other Stories** | Anton Chekhov | 1-59308-003-4 | $7.95 |
| **The Waste Land and Other Poems** | T. S. Eliot | 1-59308-279-7 | $4.95 |
| **The Way We Live Now** | Anthony Trollope | 1-59308-304-1 | $10.95 |
| **The Wind in the Willows** | Kenneth Grahame | 1-59308-265-7 | $4.95 |
| **The Wings of the Dove** | Henry James | 1-59308-296-7 | $7.95 |
| **Wives and Daughters** | Elizabeth Gaskell | 1-59308-257-6 | $7.95 |
| **The Woman in White** | Wilkie Collins | 1-59308-280-0 | $7.95 |
| **Women in Love** | D. H. Lawrence | 1-59308-258-4 | $8.95 |
| **The Wonderful Wizard of Oz** | L. Frank Baum | 1-59308-221-5 | $6.95 |
| **Wuthering Heights** | Emily Brontë | 1-59308-128-6 | $5.95 |

## BARNES & NOBLE CLASSICS

If you are an educator and would like to receive an
Examination or Desk Copy of a Barnes & Noble Classics edition,
please refer to Academic Resources on our website at
WWW.BN.COM/CLASSICS
or contact us at
BNCLASSICS@BN.COM

All prices are subject to change.